SERIES LIST

Forever Road (Book #1)

Black Opal (Book #2)

Rocks & Gravel (Book #3)

Rest Stop (Book #4)

Forbidden Highway (Book #5)

Rear View: Prequel (Book #6)

Crossroads (Book #7)

Dead End (Book #8)

Dark Traveler (Book #9)

Wrong Turn (Book #10)

Last Exit (Book #11)

REST STOP

PERI JEAN MACE GHOST THRILLERS #4

CATIE RHODES

For my sweetie.

1

───────

I reached for my iced latte, an hour old and mostly water, and fumbled it. It tipped toward the immaculate floorboard of Mysti Whitebyrd's Toyota Camry. She grabbed the paper cup before it could capsize and pushed it into my hand.

"Nervous, Peri Jean?" She turned off the radio, a relief since the Tyler-based station spat more static than music two hours north of its origin.

Nervous didn't cover it. I spent the eight years after my divorce developing my ability to do odd jobs into a lucrative business only to lose it all in the course of twenty-four hours. Venturing into uncharted career territory using my ability to communicate with the spirit world scared the life out me.

"Maybe you should let Brad do this." The few séances I'd done for Mysti's witch-for-hire business did little to make me feel prepared to contract for an actual missing persons investigator.

"Hell, no. My brother, much as I love him, doesn't have the talent to do this job." Mysti pulled her wild, sun-bleached brown hair into a butterfly clip and examined herself in the visor mirror. "He's careless, and he complains all the time. Griffin Reed insists on complete professionalism from his contractors."

What if I don't measure up? I still had hope I could use my curse to make money. Griffin Reed could dash those hopes all to hell. What then? Slinging fried chicken at a gas station?

"Stop worrying. You hear me?" She took her gaze off my face and read the road signs. "Our turnoff's coming up." She pointed at a green sign reading "Nazareth" with an arrow pointing right.

I turned onto a cracked and buckled state highway and immediately saw another sign for Nazareth. This one told me it was two miles away. I sped up to fifty-five, the posted speed limit, and took in my surroundings.

On both sides of the road, cleared pastures full of yellow, dead grass stretched far as I could see. Clusters of Black Angus cows clustered around watering tanks, waving their skinny tails against the horseflies. The land was empty. There wasn't even a convenience store. No man's land.

"Life is about taking chances. Sometimes we jump out of choice. Sometimes it's out of necessity." Mysti glanced at a slip of paper sitting in her lap. "Your part-time bartending gig, working for those bikers, can't pay much."

It didn't. Last month, after I paid for gas to drive out there and back, it paid the light bill and the propane bill. I imagined I'd have the high-speed Internet or the satellite TV cut off before too much longer.

"I'm guessing you don't have too many other options." Mysti squeezed my shoulder, maybe to let me know she meant no harm.

"You're right. The best offer I've gotten came from Benny Longstreet as his personal assistant." I grimaced, reliving the rage I felt when he asked me to come work for him, offered with a lewd wink. I knew what he wanted my assistance doing. *Not in this lifetime, donkey boy.* I'd rather eat boiled raccoon asshole, but I knew I needed paying work. Mysti's help in turning my ability to communicate with the spirit world into money was my last chance. No matter how much sense it made, I still felt like a charlatan. I never imagined it would come to this.

"See the white billboard up there?" Mysti tapped me and pointed. "Pull off in front of it. Griff wanted us to see it before we came into town."

The flaking white billboard winked in the distance. I squinted to read the faded black writing covering it but was still too far away. Sensing movement in my peripheral vision, I took my eyes off the road. Out here in North Texas farm country, hitting an animal might mean hitting a horse, a cow, or a deer. The impact could very well kill us.

At first, my mind rejected what I saw. Then a ringing buzzed in my ears. It spread until my whole head hummed with it. My stomach tried to climb out of my body via my throat. I grunted. What I saw was too weird for words.

A family of four stood on the side of the road. Mother, father, and two kids. Each member of the family wore a bloodstained burlap bag over his head. The bags had no eyeholes and were tied at the neck. The smallest member of the burlap bag head family wore a cute white dress with sunflowers on it. The dress bore dirt stains with blood dripping from its ruffled hem. She raised her hand to wave at me. Somewhere in another part of my brain a child's voice screamed in agony and fear. Sweat popped out all over me as I took in her horror and pain.

Mysti half turned to me. "Peri Jean, girl, it's right up here." She took one look at the expression on my face and leaned forward so she could see out the driver's side window. She turned back to me, lines etched into her forehead and her mouth open in horror. She saw it too. Mysti started to speak but something else caught her attention. Her eyes got even wider.

"Watch out," she screamed.

I jerked my attention back to the road and yanked the wheel. The bumper of Mysti's brand new Toyota Camry barely missed a dude riding his tractor in the middle of the fucking road. I jerked the wheel hard, hitting the gravel shoulder and fishtailing. We slid to a stop less than a foot from a barbed wire fence. I sat there gasping, heart jackhammering in my chest.

The farmer stopped his tractor in the middle of the road. He shook his fist and yelled, "The hell you doing? Slow down!"

I ignored him, closed my eyes, and took a deep breath. The calm crowded out the fear still racing through me. I opened my eyes again. In front of us was the billboard where Mysti wanted us to stop.

"See?" I turned to her. "Here we are."

My friend had her hand pressed to her chest, her eyes still wide and spooked. She shook her head at my attempt to lighten the situation.

I turned my attention to the billboard.

My daughter went missing March 28, 1980. Her name is Susan Lynn Franklin. Susie was born December 18, 1962, has blond hair and blue eyes, 5'2" and weighs 98 lbs. The State Police said she's a runaway, but I don't believe that. If you have any information, please contact Margaret (Meg) Franklin at the following address or phone number.

"This is who your PI friend wants us to look for?" I nudged Mysti.

"You know what I know," Mysti said. "Griffin Reed has his quirks, and not telling about a case until he can talk to me face to face is one of them."

Not for the first time, I took note of the way Mysti said "Griffin Reed." It made me think their relationship consisted of more than professional interest. I held back a smirk and read over the sign again. This girl, Susie Franklin, had been missing for over thirty-five years. Why try to find her after all that time? In spite of my new job jitters, I felt a little spark of curiosity.

The farmer turned his tractor around and parked it across the road from us. *Oh, boy. He wants to chew us out.* I didn't take being chewed out graciously.

The guy got off his tractor and hitched up his plain black pants, probably Dickie's. He waited for an eighteen-wheeler to pass. The wind from it ruffled his thick white hair. He crossed the road, the shine from his black work shoes catching the dull sun. I unbuckled my seatbelt and got out of the car, waiting until he got close enough to hear before I spoke.

"I sure am sorry. I thought I saw"—I paused and searched my mind for an appropriate substitute—"an animal about to dart out on the road. Been driving for a couple of hours, and I'm tired." Truth was, I was always tired these days. It plagued me like a cold I couldn't quite shake. If this old feller copped an attitude, I might give him something to remember me by. We stared at each other a few minutes. I tried to keep my expression humble and contrite. Really, I did.

"It's all right. Anywhere near that curve is always a risk." He squinted his eyes and stared at me, cocking his head to one side and glancing right at the spot where I saw the burlap head family. "You're white as a sheet, girl. You sure you're all right?"

"I'm fine. Shook up is all." I rubbed my hand over my cheek and found it covered with a clammy layer of sweat.

"Where you coming from?" He asked the question the way a country person does, completely sure of his right to know.

"South of here. Tyler."

He nodded. "You headed into Nazareth? Or going all the way to Sandal?"

"Nazareth." Mysti joined us.

The man took in Mysti's handkerchief style skirt of many colors and her fringed shawl. He raised his eyebrows and glanced down at the leather Jesus shoes she wore. He smiled.

"Heard Meggy Franklin hired some folks to find out what happened to her Susie. Y'all them?"

"Sure are. I'm Mysti Whitebyrd, and this is my associate, Peri Jean Mace." Mysti put on a big, toothy smile, but I saw the uncertainty in her brown colored eyes. She held out her hand to the old man. He took it, gave it a token squeeze, and dropped it like it might contaminate him.

"Lewis DeVoss." He glanced at Mysti and frowned before turning his gaze on me, the weight of it drifting down to my torn-up jeans and worn-out cowboy boots. He nodded, almost to himself. "Own this whole stretch o' land, both sides of the road."

"Lotta land." I didn't know what else to say. "Cows? Or crops too?"

"Mostly the cows," DeVoss said. "Some hay."

"How'd you know we were here to work the Susie Franklin case?" Mysti asked.

"Nazareth ain't got more'n eight hundred souls calling it home. We're all related or we've known each other so long we might as well be. Not much stays secret 'round these parts." He wiped at his nose. "Besides, I felt bad for poor Meggy Franklin. She's good folks."

I grew up in a small town. Maybe not as small as Nazareth, but I knew all about the way secrets don't stay secrets. This open landscape and the big sky hanging over it seemed like it wouldn't harbor secrets too happily. Feeling the old man's hard gaze on me, I glanced back at him and recoiled at the intensity of his stare.

"Give you ladies a piece o' advice, you don't mind." He

waited for us to invite him to continue, like country folks do, his arms crossed over his chest.

"Please," I said.

"Don't stay here in Nazareth too long. And don't go in no abandoned buildings. We got a dangerous element 'round here. Outsiders got a way of disappearing." His speech made, he turned to go.

"Thanks, Mr. DeVoss," I called after him, throwing a glance at Mysti. She needed to thank him too, in case we had to talk to him again. I found her frozen, her hands hanging limply at her sides, the way city people get when something scares them. DeVoss half-turned and gave me a little wave and smile. The smile never touched his eyes.

Mysti turned back to the car, but I stepped close and grabbed her arm and shook my head. Keeping my voice low, I said, "Don't let him know he spooked you. Wait for him to leave." I elbowed her. "Try not to look so damn scared."

I might as well have told her to hold her breath and count to six thousand. Everything about Mysti, from her posture to the expression on her face, screamed fear. *Can't win 'em all.*

We stood there in front of the old billboard like it held the answers to the world and watched Lewis DeVoss amble to his tractor. The old man took his time climbing up and turning the thing on. He turned back for one last wave. Then he was gone, and I strolled toward the car. Mysti tried hard not to run, and she almost made it, only jogging the last couple of steps.

"He's just unhappy a couple of outsiders are poking around," I told her.

"I know." She kept her gaze fastened on the road, jaw working. Having seen her like this a few other times, I knew to keep my mouth shut.

I got the car back on the road and drove slowly, hoping not to run into Lewis DeVoss again. We passed an overgrown rest stop with a chain across the driveway. A closed sign and a no trespassing sign hung from the chain. The hair stood up on the back of my neck. The old man's words came back to me. *Don't go in no abandoned buildings. Outsiders got a way of disappearing.*

I was glad to see the green city limits sign for Nazareth, Texas. The population listed on the sign said seven hundred fifty-seven. DeVoss had been close to right.

"This road goes straight through town." Mysti regained some of her composure. She set the cellphone on her lap and tapped on its screen. "The motel's after we pass through."

We drove through downtown Nazareth. Not much to see. The weather-beaten, faded buildings housed a few antique shops, a dollar store, and a couple of diners. Nobody walked the streets, other than a stray dog so skinny his ribs and hip bones showed. I slowed to let him pass in front of us and was struck by the feeling of being watched. I twisted in my seat, casting my gaze about, until a car came up behind us and I had to start moving again.

"This is a creepy damn place," Mysti muttered, almost to herself. "Wonder how Griff is faring here."

Again I heard the lilt in her voice when she spoke his

name. Despite my unease, I smiled. The motel, a single row of about ten rooms set a few hundred yards off the road, came up, and I pulled into the driveway. This place didn't look much better than the rest of Nazareth. The bricks needed a good pressure washing, and the asphalt parking lot was buckled and cracked. The rooms would either be so nasty they made our skin crawl or rundown but clean. I prayed for the latter and pulled into a parking place.

Here we go, I thought. I had to do the best I could and stuff my worries down deep. I hoped it was enough to impress Griffin Reed.

———

I stood in front of the car and smoked while Mysti checked us in. She emerged from the motel office holding an actual brass key. I dug my wallet out of my bag and opened it.

"No, I told you expenses are on me." Mysti walked down the single row of rooms until she came to number eight. She used the key to open the door, and the smell of old carpet rolled out to greet us.

"I'll get our bags." Maybe Mysti would leave the door open to let the room air out. I lugged our two suitcases into the room and found Mysti kissing—and I mean really kissing—a tall, wiry guy with short, slicked-down black hair and one of those sexy stubble beards. His slim cut slacks and suit jacket clashed comically with Mysti's hippie wear. I tried to back quietly out of the room, but the guy, whom I assumed was Griffin Reed, saw me and pulled away from Mysti.

"You're Peri Jean?" He held out one long-fingered hand. His fingernails had been buffed to a shine.

"Nice to you meet you, Griffin." I returned his hard handshake. He grinned. "Sorry to walk in on you guys." And I was. I missed having someone to kiss. Especially the way Mysti kissed Griffin.

"No worries, and call me Griff. My father was Griffin." He grabbed Mysti's suitcase from me and set it on the bed nearest the door. His knowing the right one amused me more than it should have, and I had to bite my cheek not to smile on my way to putting my suitcase on the bed nearest the bathroom. "Not too many places to eat in Nazareth, but I'll take y'all to an early supper. Give you ten minutes to freshen up. Meet me in the parking lot. We'll ride together." Griff gave me another smile and left the room, closing the door quietly behind him.

"I'm sorry I didn't tell you we were a thing." Mysti opened her suitcase and grabbed a little plastic zippered bag. "I was sort of afraid you wouldn't want to come, and I wanted you to do this with me so you could see how satisfying it is to make money with your gift."

You mean my curse? I already knew not to say those words to Mysti. They pushed her hot button.

"Why on earth would I not want to meet your boyfriend?" I saw an ashtray sitting on the particle board dresser and took out my cigarettes and showed them to Mysti. She nodded and went into the bathroom and turned on the light. I lit up and followed her, pulling myself up to sit on the long sink vanity.

"Because you're lonely, whether you want to admit it or not." She glanced up from applying her lip gloss and raised her eyebrows. "Plus, he's not really my boyfriend. Commitment issues, I think."

"Too bad. He's cute." I winked at her.

"He really is." She giggled and finished putting on her makeup. "Griff'll want to work after supper. We might be interviewing people. Make yourself presentable."

I touched up my makeup and brushed my chin-length hair, staring hard at the black for strands of gray, but didn't change out of my worn-in jeans and beat-up cowboy boots. I bet I'd fit in better than Griff and Mysti did.

We found Griff standing next to a new gray SUV, smoking a cigarillo. He stubbed it out and hurried to open the door for Mysti. Without asking where we wanted to go, he drove us to a diner called Family Home Cooking. The sign out front promised all we could eat fried catfish. We had to circle the full lot several times before someone pulled out, and we snagged their spot.

Griff opened the door for Mysti and went around the SUV's back and pulled out a black canvas messenger bag. We walked into the restaurant, a large, open room lined with booths. Tables created an obstacle course through the middle of the room. Every head in the restaurant turned to stare at us.

Most of Family Home Cooking's patrons wore about the same thing I did. Mysti and Griff stood out like a pair of chess pieces on a checkerboard. A young woman wearing a tight, white T-shirt with Family Home Cooking emblazoned on the front hurried over to us.

"Folks, there's a booth about to open up over in that corner." She raised one arm to point, and her shirt pulled up, exposing a fish-belly white roll of fat hanging over her jeans. She left the T-shirt the way it was and went on about her business, leaving us to stand like vultures while the elderly couple occupying the booth she pointed out slowly stood and gathered their belongings and finally sauntered off, the woman staring hard at us as they passed. We slid into the booth even though the other couple's ketchup-smeared plates and half-empty tea glasses still sat on it.

"What y'all want to drink?" A middle-aged woman appeared next to the booth and took out an order pad.

"Do you have beer?" Griff didn't sound or look too hopeful.

"Nowhere in Nazareth has beer. Hall County's dry as a bone." She delivered the speech in a bored monotone. "We got iced-tea, sweet or unsweet and all kinds of Coke."

"Water?" I didn't trust the tea, and soft drinks were too sweet for me.

She scribbled on her notepad without answering.

Mysti and Griff ordered unsweet tea.

"Catfish buffet's all there is. Go over to the steam counter and tell 'em what you want. Price is $11.99 per person." She turned to walk away.

"Ma'am?" Griff called after her. She turned back, her mouth still set in the same grim line. "Can we get the table cleaned off?"

She heaved out the kind of sigh only the truly put

upon know how to deliver. "I'll have it done by the time you get back with your plates."

Turned out, she didn't and had to rush over and remove the plates and glasses while we stood there holding our food. Griff had to ask her not to take away the drinks she'd brought for us. We ate our food in silence. When we finished, Griff ordered coffee and pulled a laptop and a few files out of his messenger bag.

"As you probably guessed from the billboard, we're here to look into the disappearance of Susan Franklin." He pushed a button to power up his laptop and pushed it against the wall so it faced outward. He tapped a few buttons and a grainy newspaper photo of a smiling girl looked out at us.

"Why after so many years?" I stared at the face, knowing she was probably dead, probably a horrible death.

"Let's let this young lady serve our coffee, and I'll tell you a little story."

The girl with the muffin top set out a thermal carafe of coffee. Then she dug in her apron and set down the bill. Rather than leaving, she stood, staring at us expectantly, until Griff picked up the bill, dug in his wallet, and handed her some bills with a smile. "Keep the change."

The girl's small mouth dropped open, and she drew in a deep breath. "Thanks a lot, mister." She made a big show of dragging the little sugar holder to the middle of the table and giving us a toothy smile before she walked off. Griff said nothing until she was out of earshot.

"Susie was a senior at Nazareth High. Good student,

track runner. She dropped out of high school midway through the fall semester of her senior year." Griff poured coffee into thick off-white mugs. "We have an appointment to speak with her mother in a few minutes. I'm going to let her tell you why Susie quit school."

After the ordeal at the billboard outside Nazareth, Griff's insistence on not telling us the whole story grated on me. "Why don't you just tell us?"

"Good question. What happened to Susan Franklin was fairly well-documented in the news media. It was a huge scandal." He stopped to take a sip of his coffee. "But I've never heard her mother tell her version of events. Since neither you nor Mysti have heard any of Susie's story, I'm hoping one of you will hear anything I skim over because it sounds familiar. The small details are what breaks cases like this wide open."

I was tired of being in the dark, but I nodded. I'd get paid either way.

"Now let's get down to what I really want the two of you to know. I found out about Susie Franklin while looking into another missing person's case." Griff pulled a sheet of paper from his file and slid it across the table to Mysti and me. A picture of a smiling girl took up most of the sheet. Underneath her picture were the words "$150,000 reward for any information on the whereabouts of Kaitlyn Summers who went missing September 16, 2011."

There's the real money and the reason he's willing to hire not one, but two, paranormal princesses.

"I called the number on the flyer." Griff leaned forward, chest pressing into the hard edge of the table, intent on his story and earnest about telling it. "Talked to Kaitlyn's father. Nice guy. He said the last time he talked to Kaitlyn, she had turned off the main road because she saw a sign for a rest stop. She apparently needed a restroom."

I shivered at the mention of the rest stop. Surely Kaitlyn didn't stop at the one Mysti and I passed earlier. It looked too run down and the vegetation too overgrown to have been open in 2011. *Stay out of abandoned buildings.*

Griff took in my shiver. "She lost signal not long afterward, and he never spoke to her again."

"Law enforcement find anything?" My ex was the new sheriff of the county where I lived. I learned during our time together that law enforcement got involved in everything.

"Not even her car. Her cellphone last pinged off a tower near here." Griff stopped talking as a family of four passed our booth. "Thing is, when I started looking into Summers's disappearance, I learned something funny. Somewhere between forty and fifty people have gone missing in the last thirty years, within a twenty-mile radius of where we're sitting." He tapped the table for emphasis.

Outsiders have a way of disappearing. The skin on my back crawled.

"Something's going on here, has been going on for a while. If I can, I intend to find out what it is." Griff glanced between Mysti and me. "The reward'll be nice, but this'll help a lot of families find closure."

"And get your name on the map." I smiled to let him know I didn't think ill of him for it.

"You bet." He pointed one long finger at me. "Get you ladies on the map, too. Maybe lead to some business."

He and Mysti high-fived. Watching them made me feel good. Even if Griff wouldn't commit, they seemed to have a good deal going. Another thing I learned from my abortive relationship with Dean Turgeau was the importance of recognizing when things worked and ending them right away if they didn't.

"Do you think whatever's doing this is something paranormal?" It sounded more like human evil to me, like we might be sitting in a serial killer's favorite hunting spot.

"I just don't know." Griff caressed his stubble beard and shook his head. "Mysti told me you're a powerful medium. I hoped, if nothing else, you'd be able to contact Susie's spirit."

The burlap head family popped back into my mind, and I quickly told Griff about seeing them. He shuffled through his papers and showed me a newspaper report about a family moving cross-country in the days before cellphones who vanished somewhere between the Louisiana border and Dallas.

"This them?" He tapped a photo of a family smiling in front of an old RV.

"I didn't see their faces." I picked up the paper and scanned through it, noticing a PI hired by the family found a truck stop waitress north of Tyler who remembered them coming into the place where she worked. She said the little girl's dress had sunflowers on it. I handed the paper back to Griff. It trembled along with my hand.

The middle-aged waitress marched over to our table

and loomed over us like a schoolmarm who'd caught a bunch of kids smoking behind the wood shop.

"We close in ten minutes." She bit out the words as though she'd have rather screamed them and marched away.

"We need to get to Margaret Franklin's anyway," Griff told us. Mysti and I helped him pack up his things and got out before Miss Meanypants returned.

2

Griff drove us through a maze of narrow, blacktopped streets. Trees hung in a canopy over the road. The dying sunlight streaked through the branches, dappling light and shadows in front of us. He pulled to the curb in front of a tall, skinny Queen Anne style Victorian with a for sale sign in front.

Despite the sunny yellow and sage paint, obviously fresh, and the brighter than bright white picket fence, a pall hung over the house. The house itself seemed to sit alone and apart from the other tidy houses on the street. It seemed like the loneliest kid in school, which I knew more than a little about.

Griff held open the picket fence gate for Mysti and me and followed us up the walk and onto a tiny, rounded front porch. A hanging bench swing took up most of the space. He edged past us to knock on the front door, the white columns on either side dwarfing him. The light fixtures set into the columns were already lit to welcome the oncoming darkness.

From inside the house, soft, quick footsteps approached the huge door. It swung open, and we stood face to face with a white-haired woman wearing paint-stained blue jeans and a matching T-shirt. Her canvas shoes must have started out white, but dirt and stains had turned them the color of dishwater. She struggled to smile but never got both sides of her lips to cooperate and finally settled on a kind of grimace.

"Griffin Reed?" She settled her gaze on each of us in turn, lingering the longest on me.

"Call me Griff." He held out his hand for her to shake, which she did after staring at it for a while.

"Y'all come on in, I guess." She held open the door for us to pass.

The house's interior was as smartly spiffed up as its outside. I thought I smelled the scent of refinished wood floors and fresh paint. The bannister on the stairs to the second floor held my attention the longest. The wood's rich, flawless stain gleamed in the lamplight, casting the room into a golden-hazed shadow world. Despite how pretty everything looked, the same sadness permeated the rooms. I glanced at Griff and Mysti and saw they'd locked hands, both their faces set in grim discomfort. The right buyer for this wonderful home would be a long time coming.

"Come on in my office." Margaret Franklin led us down a narrow hallway off the foyer, moving faster and more gracefully than I'd have imagined a woman her age capable.

As I passed in front of the beautiful stairway, I saw the outline of someone sitting on the top step, arms hunched over her legs, the glow of evening sun glimmering over a headful of blond hair. *Must be Susie Franklin's ghost.* Maybe she would be willing to communicate with me. Some spirits resisted. I hoped she wouldn't be one of them.

Margaret Franklin showed us into her office. The narrow room, with its tall windows and white painted brick fireplace, might have originally served as a parlor. She motioned us to sit on a worn leather couch positioned in front of a bank of filing cabinets. I sat on one end, next to Mysti, and Griff sat on the other end. The freshly painted walls were naked, but posters of Susie, most of them emblazoned with the word missing, lay everywhere. They must have been the former decor. Margaret watched me looking around.

"Can I get y'all Cokes or anything?"

"No, but thank you." Mysti said. "We came from eating supper."

Margaret rolled an old-fashioned wooden desk chair in front of the couch and sat in it, her gaze finding me again. "I know you," she said finally. "You're Peri Jean Mace from Gaslight City."

My cheeks got hot. I squirmed on the couch, looking for a comfortable position and not finding one. "Yes, I am."

"I agreed to hire a private detective, not a psychic." Margaret glared at Griff.

"Her fees come out of mine. There won't be any extra charges." Griff's face remained impassive.

I wanted to know how Margaret knew who I was, what I was. Had I been on my own, I'd have asked. No, demanded. This situation, working for Griff, required I shake it off. I did so reluctantly.

Margaret focused on Mysti. "And you, little miss tie-dye hippie, what's your part?"

"I have a business specializing in séances, among other things. I'm here to assist Peri Jean if she needs it." Mysti said the words in an even, professional tone I envied and wanted to learn how to emulate. I had to find it within myself to do this, to make this work. It was my last chance before I started wearing a uniform and a name tag to work.

"I'm glad you didn't tell me you were bringing these two," Margaret told Griff. "I'd have probably told you not to bother. You've got to understand, after Susie went missing, I got hit on by every crackpot in the country. Folks claiming to be psychics would call me up." A shot of anger crossed over her features. "At first I was really gullible."

"I'm sorry if you were swindled," Griff said. "I assure you I am honest. The rate I quoted you won't go up. Sometimes I do employ traditional investigative methods. On a case this old, however, the trail is cold. Mysti and Peri Jean might give me the advantage I need to help you. Are you ready to talk about Susie? Maybe tell me what your dream outcome to all this is?"

Margaret nibbled on her bottom lip for several seconds. Her eyes clouded with some sort of internal debate. Finally, her face hardened, and she spoke. "I'm sure you saw the for sale sign out front. This town is full of bad memories for me. I'm retired, and I want to move on. Before I do, I want to find my baby's remains and give her the burial she deserves."

"We will do our best to help you achieve that goal." Griff pulled his messenger bag into his lap and dug out some papers. "This is a standard contract for my services. Why don't you look it over, sign it. Then I'd like you tell us everything you know about Susie's disappearance."

Margaret put on a set of reading glasses and pored over each page of the contract, brow furrowed. She got to the last page and sat there chewing on her lip and staring at it. Drawing a deep breath, as though fortifying herself, she scribbled her name. She held out the papers to Griff, and he slipped them back into his messenger bag. He took out a small, digital recorder.

"Do you mind if I record our conversation? I use the recording to make my notes."

Margaret waved off the question, nodding. "I suppose I should tell you this ain't my first experience with a private investigator."

"That so?" Griff leaned forward, his handsome face set in concerned lines, gaze fixed on Margaret.

"I hired Phil Cotton out of Dallas. You ever heard of him?"

"Actually, I have. He was one of the first people I met when I started doing this work. He and the guy who trained me were like those old-style TV gumshoes." Griff chuckled.

Margaret nodded, allowing herself a small smile.

"How soon after Susie's disappearance did you hire Mr. Cotton?"

"Within a month. The police force wouldn't help me look for her. They said it was because she ran away, but it was really because of her trouble here in town." Anger flared in her eyes and cheeks, and she shook it off with an air of resignation I knew by heart.

"Did Phil learn anything useful? I'm sorry to say he died several years ago, and I have no idea if I could get my hands on his records. Anything you remember would be a great help."

"I got his report in one of those file cabinets behind you." Margaret stood, walked around the couch, and began opening and closing drawers. I twisted in my seat to watch her. She took out a yellowed file and handed it to Griff.

"Phil checked area restaurants, bus stations, the like. Nobody'd seen her. It was like she walked out of this house and fell off the edge of the earth." Margaret sat back down in her rolling chair.

Remembering Griff's similar comment about the other disappearances, I shivered. Margaret watched me, her eyebrows knitting together. She turned back to Griff.

"You told me when you contacted me you'd found Susie's website and then did some research. What do you know about the circumstances surrounding her disappearance?"

"Just what the newspapers printed at the time," Griff said. "I'd like to hear you tell me everything you remember. Mysti and Peri know nothing about Susie's disappearance, so please start from the beginning for their benefit."

Margaret's face twisted. She opened her mouth, closed it, and opened it again. "Susie's father was a long-haul truck driver who got killed in an accident when Susie was starting high school. He didn't have insurance, and he hung on for about six weeks on life support. His death ate up everything we'd put away to send Susie to college." She spoke the words as though she'd either said them often or thought them often. I'd guess both. She took a deep breath and started speaking again. "I encouraged Susie to find something she could use to get a scholarship to college. We'd gotten a new football coach, and he started a girl's track program. He was outgoing and good-looking, and Susie signed up. She ended up running track all through high school." She sucked her upper lip into her mouth and mashed her bottom teeth into it, staring at us as though deciding whether or not she could stand to continue.

"Margaret, you're not to blame for what happened." Griff leaned forward as far as he could and stared hard at her. "None of us here will judge you."

Her expression dulled. I suspected it didn't matter if we judged her or not. She did a fine job of it herself. "The summer between Susie's junior and senior year, she changed." Margaret narrowed her eyes at the memory.

"How did your daughter change?" Mysti asked in her soft, gentle voice.

"She was thin from running track, but she got down-right skinny. And she didn't act like herself. My daughter was always bubbly and giggling. That year, she got quiet." Margaret put her hand over her mouth. "She wanted to quit track. God damn me to Hell, I wouldn't let her, and I never even asked why." She spoke the last words in a trembling, weepy voice and had to stop. She dabbed at her eyes with a tissue. "First week of October, I came home early from work and found Susie face down on her bed. She'd taken an overdose of sleeping pills. I rushed her to old Doc Rasmussen's office, and he saved her." The older woman's mouth puckered as though she'd tasted something awful. "Next day she told me she'd been sleeping with the coach since the end of her junior year."

"Oh no," Mysti whispered. Fury stormed inside me, and I pushed it down, forcing myself to stay calm.

"I took all the right steps." Margaret counted off on her fingers. "I reported him to the principal. I'm not sure what I'd been expecting, but I wasn't prepared for what happened." Her gaze settled on the floor, weighted down with events thirty-five years dead. She slumped with the burden of it. "See, the coach—Bobby John Culpepper— was good at his job. We'd had winning seasons ever since he hired on. Principal Thomas didn't want to do anything at all. Oh, he offered to pay for Susie to go to boarding school in Dallas."

I ground my teeth. I knew all too well how small town people could band together to sweep undesirable events or people under the rug.

"What happened then?" I didn't like the grit in my voice, knew I couldn't let it get the better of me, but I had to know how this awful story ended up.

"I—I got angry. I contacted the Dallas media and hired a lawyer. The story broke, and the school suspended the coach." Margaret twisted her hands in her lap. "But, see, it didn't end there. Folks in town were mad because they thought I was trying to take away their winning ticket. None of Susie's friends would talk to her. The football team terrorized her. It was like she'd done something terrible. I suppose, to all of them, she had. She stood it for a few weeks and quit going to school."

None of us said anything for several minutes. I listened to the hum of electronics in the house and thought about Susie Franklin.

"Tell us about the day Susie disappeared," said Griff, voice soft and full of sympathy. "Was there any sign of a struggle?"

"No. I came home from work, and she was gone. She'd taken a few clothes, her duffle bag, and her purse. I never found her babysitting money, so I guess she had that on her, too." Margaret drew in a trembling breath.

"It's your opinion she left on her own will?" Griff's voice never wavered from its sympathetic croon.

"Yes, she ran away." Margaret threw up her hands. "But Susie would have called me once she got where she was going. Or sometime over the years. She'd have never left me hanging. She knew I loved her, but I was the postmistress over at the post office. Moving to another town would have meant starting over, maybe a pay cut. We had no savings." Margaret's voice rose with each declaration, and her eyes shone with tears.

"What became of the coach?" Mysti put her elbows on her knees and leaned forward.

"With Susie gone, what little investigation there was died." Bitterness crept into Margaret's voice. "Coach Bobby

John took the rest of that year off, but he was back the next year coaching the Nazareth High School Fighting Tigers to another winning season."

Hurt welled up in my chest and closed my throat. What an awful thing for this poor woman to have to watch.

Margaret got up and walked to the antique desk behind her. She dug through the drawers and put a few things in a plastic grocery sack. "Mr. Reed? Since you've hired psychics, maybe I should give these to you."

Griff rose from the couch and took the sack from her, briefly glancing at its contents. To my surprise, he held it out to me. I peeked inside. Inside was a school picture of Susie Franklin. Susie had her white-blond hair styled into Farrah Fawcett waves and wore blue eye shadow to set off her cornflower blue eyes. Griff didn't sit back down but instead nodded to Mysti and me. We stood.

"I think we've got enough, Margaret." He held out his hand again, and she took it briefly. She turned to me.

"I put Susie's track shirt in there so y'all could remember she was really a person, one who was done wrong by this town."

"I will do my best to settle this for you," I said.

We left the house in silence and drove through dark streets back to the motel.

———

"I FEEL funny dumping you in here by yourself." Mysti leaned against the standard hotel room vanity, its edge cutting off the head of the peacock on her white kimono, and piled her hair on top of her head. She flipped on the two curling irons on the counter and glanced at me in the mirror.

"Don't. How often do you two actually get to spend time together?" The elaborateness of her beauty ritual both amused me and made me feel incredibly lonely. I didn't miss Dean so much as I missed having someone to share life with. No matter how awful I felt, I'd break my own back not to let it show. Mysti didn't deserve to have her evening with Griff ruined with my drama.

"Not often." Mysti waved the eyeliner applicator in her hand. "Well, I suspect it's often enough for Griff."

"Why do you stay interested if you don't want the same thing?" Actually, I knew the answer to this one. Sometimes a guy seems worth jumping through extra hoops in case there's a chance it might work out.

"I keep hoping he'll wake up some day." She applied thick, black cat eyes and put away the eyeliner. "Griff got married young and divorced after a couple of years. He thinks the problems had to do with his personality flaws."

"And he thinks the same things'll go wrong if you two get serious?"

Mysti nodded and stroked mascara onto her eyelashes. "I don't think it was his fault. It was being too young, too poor, and desperately unhappy because of those things."

"From what you can gather."

"I keep forgetting you went through a nasty breakup not so long ago." She stopped patting glittery powder over her face long enough to give me a sympathetic smile.

"I'm sure not one to give relationship advice." I leaned

over the counter and picked up a pot of plum colored eye shadow. I'd never have the nerve to wear something so bold, but it fit Mysti.

"You want to, though. It's written all over your face." She pulled her hair out of its clip and grabbed the larger of the two curling irons.

"Dean taught me firmly held beliefs don't change. No matter how much either of you want them to." I unscrewed the lid off the plum colored eyeshadow and took the eye shadow brush Mysti handed me. I slid off the counter so I could see my reflection and started applying it. I couldn't help myself, even though I knew I wouldn't like it. "My advice is to either enjoy the status quo, knowing it'll never be more, or tell him what you want and see where he stands. Be willing to end it if what he says doesn't make you happy."

Mysti said nothing and picked up the smaller curling iron. She used it to make tiny ringlets framing her face. She unplugged both curling irons and stared at me in the mirror. "That what you wish you'd done with Dean?"

"Sort of. I wish I had accepted his limitations regarding who and what I am a lot earlier on than I did." A more truthful wish was never having taken up with him in the first place. I could have saved myself the grief.

"At least you're no worse for the wear. And look at you starting something new using your special talent." She winked at me and gave my hair a tug. "You've even got this new look going with your longer hair. You got the world by the balls." She grabbed her clothes off their hangers, went into the tiny bathroom, and closed the door.

I listened to her rustle around dressing and thought about what I was doing here in Nazareth, Texas. What if I was making another stupid mistake, like with Dean? Just as Dean hadn't been my dream man, medium-for-hire was not my dream job.

Cleaning houses and mowing lawns wasn't either, remember? No, it wasn't. I learned to look for the positives in the work. Many of the positives of being a medium-for-hire would be the same. Not having to show up and sit behind a desk or stand behind a counter eight hours a day. Choosing my own clientele. Working with different people all the time.

But what if it doesn't work out? What's next? I didn't know, and not knowing scared me. Too much in my life had changed over the last year, and none of the changes were happy ones. People I loved were dead. I knew secrets I never wanted to know.

"You *can* do this." Mysti's voice came from right next to my ear. I yelped and tripped over my own feet, adrenaline surging through my bloodstream.

"I didn't even hear you come out of the bathroom." I sat down on my bed and took in her outfit, unable to keep my eyes from widening.

Mysti posed for me, sticking her knee through the slit in her floor-length, black, slinky nightgown. She twisted and turned on her strappy, black, and high-heeled, do-me shoes.

"Wow. He won't know what hit him." I shook my head.

Mysti waved off my compliment. "Sorry I surprised you. You were so deep in thought and worry, somebody needed to break you out of it." She stood in front of me and met my gaze. "You can do this. Really. But keep one thing in mind. It's your choice. If you really don't want to, I'll take you to the bus station in the morning. But since we're playing girlfriends and giving advice, here's mine to you. Give this a chance, a really fair one. Quit worrying and put your heart into it." She headed for the door, reached for it, and then turned back. "You really think I look all right?"

"I think you could stop traffic." I gave her a little wave and watched her step out into the night. A few seconds later, I heard her rap on Griff's door and his appreciative exclamation as he opened it. The loneliness surged over me again. Mysti had left her car keys and instructions to take it out if I decided to.

The idea was tempting. On the way into Nazareth, I remembered seeing a little honkytonk. It was twenty or so miles south of town. As quickly as I had the idea, I dismissed it. I spent most of my twenties on learning the art of the disposable relationship. I'd either grown out of it or lost my taste for it. *Nah.* Maybe sometime. But not tonight.

I should take Mysti's advice and throw myself into this work. The plastic grocery sack Margaret Franklin gave me sat on the cheap dresser. I pushed myself off the bed, grabbed the sack, and took it to the little two chair table by the window. One by one, I removed the items inside.

I set the school picture of Susie Franklin on the table where I could look at it. She didn't look much like the cowering, thin ghost I saw sitting on the top stair in

Margaret's house. I stared hard at the picture, at Susie's happy blue eyes, at the tilt of her head. She was looking at someone off camera. Maybe the coach Margaret said Susie claimed to have an affair with?

The next item I pulled from the bag was Susie's track shirt. It was a simple white T-shirt—no microfiber or fancy materials back in 1980—with the words Nazareth Girls Track Team printed on it in red letters. I set it aside on the table and grabbed for the next item, which was a hard object wrapped in newspaper. Margaret hadn't mentioned this.

I unwrapped the newspaper, careful not to tear it, and found myself holding an inexpensive souvenir snow globe, the kind with the cheap plastic base. This one advertised Reno, Nevada. *Why would Margaret include this? Was it a favorite trinket of Susie's?* I glanced back at the track shirt. Margaret told me about the track shirt and why she included it. Why didn't she tell me about the snow globe?

Next door, Mysti and Griff must have dispensed with the preliminaries and gotten down to business. They themselves weren't loud. But the headboard banging against the wall was. Sitting there listening made me feel like a nasty, voyeuristic intruder. Mysti said I could use her car, said to put my best effort into doing this job. I was going to do it. I grabbed the car keys and the room key and slipped out as quietly as I could.

A few minutes later, I parked the car at Margaret Franklin's curb. The lights were on in the house, but I sat behind the wheel, doubting my decision to come over here. Margaret might resent me intruding on her a second time. I picked up the snow globe and held it up to the dim light coming into the car from the streetlight. I still didn't see the significance. I turned my gaze back to the house. Someone stood from the swing on the porch.

My heart went into overdrive, stealing my breath away. I put my hand on the key, still plugged into the ignition, and started to turn it. Then Margaret stepped out onto the steps leading up to the porch. I couldn't make out the expression on her face, but she had her hand clutched at the neckline of her shirt. She deserved to know who was here at the very least. I got out of the car, still holding the globe in my hand.

"It's Peri Jean Mace, Mrs. Franklin." I called in a low voice.

"I was sitting out here enjoying the night. Would you like to join me?"

There was no answer but yes. I trudged up the steps and sat next to her on the swing. She turned to me, ready to say something, and gasped.

"Where'd you get that?"

"It was in the sack you sent."

"No, ma'am, it wasn't." Her voice rose. She took a deep breath, as though calming herself. When she spoke again, her voice went back to normal volume. "I promise you I didn't put it in the sack. I haven't seen that thing, well, since Susie disappeared. I don't really know when it was gone, just that I never found it again."

I held out the globe to her, but she wouldn't take it.

"No. Maybe Susie wanted you to have it."

I cradled the globe in my hands. Maybe she was right,

although that thought gave me a shiver. "You seemed unhappy earlier about Griff hiring a—what was your word?—a psychic. Now you think Susie's ghost made sure I got this. Isn't that what you're saying?"

Margaret leaned back on the swing, letting her head fall backward. "I was an ass. I'm sorry. The way I reacted to seeing you was really a reaction to the reminder Susie is dead, not doubt of your powers."

"How do you know I see the dead?" Now was my chance to find out how she knew me. I'd be dipped in double doo-doo before I let it pass.

"I visited Gaslight City a year or so ago." She glanced at me. "My retirement from the Postal Service was coming up fast, and I briefly entertained the idea of turning this place into a bed and breakfast." She folded her hands in her lap. "Doing a little market research, I guess."

I leaned back and crossed my arms over my chest, hoping it was too dark for her to see the sea of unease churning inside me. Lots of people in my hometown thought bad stuff about me. No telling what Margaret heard.

"I stayed in a different bed and breakfast every night. The last one, the one called Gardenia's Rest, had a cocktail hour. You served."

"Don't tell me I spilled your drink on you." This conversation dug painful claws into my pride. Those little jobs used to make up a livelihood for me. They were lost to me forever because of my ability to see ghosts.

"No, you were very good. But after you left..." She trailed off and squirmed. "One of the other guests told me about you. She was about your age, had moved away, and was in town for a wedding or something. Said her cousin died under odd circumstances. Family thought he'd been murdered. You stopped by her aunt and uncle's house one day and told them what happened to him. I think she said it was some kind of freak accident."

I dug my elbows into my knees, putting all the weight I could on them to distract myself from the sick feeling building in my stomach. I remembered the situation well and still felt the burn of embarrassment over the way those people looked at me. Disgusted, yet curious. It reminded me of the way Dean looked at me the day he dumped me. I couldn't look at Margaret and regretted coming here. This was a mistake, all of it. I stared at the snow globe in my lap, focusing on it until it was all I saw. Distantly, I felt the black opal I wore around my neck heating up the way it always did in response to my otherness asserting itself.

The snow globe lit up from the inside, but the snow and the skyscape of Reno I'd seen back in my cheap motel room was gone, replaced by the inside of Margaret Franklin's house. Only this version of Margaret's house looked lived in and loved with outdated wallpaper, shag carpet, and cheap furniture mixed in with the antiques. Late afternoon sunlight streaked in through the windows. The vision built itself around me, erasing the real world piece by piece.

3

—————

I stared into the world inside the snow globe, and it became more real each second. I smelled something cooking in the kitchen. Pot roast and carrots maybe. A doorbell rang.

My insides jolted at the sound, almost pulling me out of the vision. How did I hear that? My visions were usually like silent movies.

The black opal sent a little shock of magic into my skin as though saying, "Yeah, I made that happen for you."

But the black opal didn't do it all by itself. My work with Mysti, learning from her, changed the game. Changed me. Mysti kept telling me practice would awaken more magic than I ever imagined I had. Hearing the doorbell, such a small thing, proved her right.

What else lay under the surface? Only miles traveled on this road would tell me. The important thing was I *could.* For all the things I failed at, I could get good at this with some effort.

Now concentrate, idiot. So I did, with joy. I made the inside of the snow globe my whole world.

Footsteps pounded upstairs. A tiny version of Susie, her blond hair shining in the light, appeared at the top of the staircase I'd so admired earlier in the day. She started down the staircase, and my consciousness sank into her, seeing the world through her eyes.

Susie's pale, freckled hand gripped the bannister, and I felt the cool wood sliding beneath her palm. I felt her excitement about whoever might be at the door. I couldn't exactly read her mind, but I read her emotions, and they were the ones most girls feel over some undeserving guy. She stopped to look in a mirror mounted on the wall, pushing her hair behind her ears and checking her teeth for food. She went to the door and opened it. Her bowels went loose as soon as she saw who was there.

The woman's dark blond hair hung in sloppy disarray, and she had a food stain on her shirt. She slammed one hand into Susie's chest and shoved her way inside.

Susie's scalp tingled, and she raised her arms to protect herself. My fighting instinct took over, and I tried to curl Susie's hands into fists, to help her bloody this bitch's nose. Susie's hands stayed splayed open in front of her while the woman screamed in her face.

I strained to hear the words the other woman said, but apparently I still had a lot to learn about doing this kind of thing. The fury contorting her face told me a good bit about her words. A plain gold band flashed on her third finger as she raised her left hand and slapped Susie's face.

She grabbed Susie's shirt, yanking her close, saliva frothing at the corners of her mouth as she raved.

Suddenly, the woman let go of Susie and turned away from her, bending at her waist. I couldn't see anything Susie didn't see, and it seemed to take her forever to turn her gaze to whatever interrupted the confrontation. Susie's attacker knelt on the floor next to a crying toddler. She stroked the child's hair, trying to smile and say soothing words. The child held out his arms, and the crazy woman scooped him up and carried him toward the front door. She turned back to glare at Susie and spoke three words, her teeth bared like an animal's. I didn't hear her words, but what she said was impossible to mistake.

This isn't over.

Some force jerked me out of Susie's body, turning my stomach upside down in the process. The vision around me brightened then faded like a magazine left too long in the hot Texas sun.

I came to, slumped on the wooden planks of the porch floor. At my back I heard Margaret's high, panicked voice.

"I don't know, Griff. She slumped over on the floor. I checked her pulse, and she's still alive, but not moving."

I struggled to my knees and put one arm on the porch swing so I could push myself up.

"I'm all right, Mrs. Franklin."

Margaret's mouth dropped open. "She's up. Says she's all right." She listened for a second. "Okay. I'll tell her."

"Griff and Mysti are coming to pick you up. They said to stay put."

It couldn't have taken more than ten minutes for Griff and Mysti to drive up in Griff's SUV, but it seemed like ten hours. Margaret, in full mother mode, offered me everything from hot chocolate to Vicodin. I accepted a glass of cold water to get her to go in the house and leave me alone to think.

I had a fair idea who attacked Susie at her home, but I didn't want to repeat myself. My jaunt as Susie's silent shadow cost me a lot of energy. I felt as drained as if I'd spent the day mowing lawns in hundred-degree heat.

Griff's SUV finally appeared at the curb. Mysti barely let the SUV roll to a stop before she vaulted out. She'd traded her sexy black nightie for the clothes she'd worn all day. Mouth set in a grim line and hands curled into loose fists, she marched toward me like someone going to war. Griff hurried after her, his messenger bag at his side.

"You saw something." Mysti squinted at me and sniffed the air. She leaned down and sniffed at me. "What kind of perfume are you wearing?"

"I don't wear perfume." I recoiled from Mysti, wanting to shove her away but not quite daring.

"I know." She turned to Griff. "Have you ever smelled this before? There's something familiar about it."

Griff leaned down to sniff me. "I don't even smell what you're talking about."

Margaret came close and sniffed me. She gasped. "That's Susie's perfume. Love's Baby Soft. I'll never forget the smell." Her gaze moved from my face to Mysti's. "But I threw out every bottle after Susie wasn't here anymore. Couldn't stand it."

"Mrs. Franklin—" I began.

"Oh, call me Margaret, hon."

"Margaret, do you have lawn chairs where Mysti and Griff can sit? Or would you like to go inside?"

"There's two folding chairs leaning against the railing." She pointed.

Griff got both chairs and set them up. He and Mysti sat.

I told them what I saw through Susie's eyes, every detail I could remember.

"What did the woman say?" Griff held out his recorder to me.

"Peri Jean doesn't hear their voices," Mysti said. "Her gift doesn't work that way."

"No, I still don't hear words, but I heard the doorbell this time." I searched for Mysti's gaze, eager to see her reaction.

"Oooh, really?" Mysti sat a little straighter. "So what else did you—"

Griff gave her a gentle tap on the shoulder and glared at her.

She gave me a nod and mouthed, *Later*.

"Well, what did the woman look like?" Margaret's brow furrowed. She probably wanted to get back to talking about her daughter—the reason she hired us.

"She had a full head of hair. It was the kind of blond that's really just blond on the ends. There's a lot of darker hair mixed in." I closed my eyes. The woman's anger kept me from accurately describing her face. "Good figure. Nice boobs. But she wasn't very well put together. Her pants were old, and she had a food stain on her shirt."

"But she wasn't a kid, like someone from Susie's class," Mysti said.

Slowly, I shook my head.

"Just a minute. I'll be right back." Margaret got up and went inside the house, closing the door behind her.

"I'm sorry," I said to both Griff and Mysti. "I found this snow globe in the sack Margaret gave us. She didn't mention it, and I wanted to see why she included it."

"Any break's a good break," Griff said.

Mysti stared at me, no longer really angry but definitely put out at having her romantic evening ruined.

Margaret came back out of the house holding a thin book. She flipped a light switch just inside the door and the lights on either side of the front door and an overhead light blazed to life. Now I could see the book was a school yearbook from 1978.

"I had to look through a couple to find what I was looking for, but I knew I remembered this picture." She flipped to a marked page and showed us a black and white photo of an adult couple posing in front of a display reading Senior Prom 1978. Both wore broad, joking smiles. The first thing I noticed on the woman was her huge, pregnant belly. I took the book from Margaret and held it close to my face. Now I recognized the square jaw and the Nordic cheekbones.

"It's her." I kept the book. "This must be Coach Bobby John?"

Margaret frowned and nodded. I took in Susie's love interest. I could see the attraction, especially for a teenage girl. Twenty-five-years-old, tops. Full lips and heavy brows. And those smoldering eyes.

Dark and brooding, there was some sexy mystery there, the kind a teenage girl couldn't resist. She'd be the one to take away whatever haunted this man. She'd be the one to uncover his mysteries. She'd be the last one he admired. But it never turned out just so. Guys like that got all the pussy in the world, and Susie Franklin would have been disposable to him, a fancy he may not have indulged with five more years' wisdom under his belt.

I turned my attention again to Coach Bobby John's wife, imagined her with a couple more years on her and the added fatigue of child rearing. Then I imagined how she'd look if she were a wife whose husband was having an affair with a teenager in a town where she was, for all intents and purposes, an outsider. Her behavior, while wildly inappropriate, wasn't unjustified. There was no way I'd share my thoughts with Margaret sitting right there, so I stared at the picture some more. Something new occurred to me. "This is the woman I saw in my vision, but there's something else familiar about her. I can't quite place it."

"Y'all said you went out to supper tonight. Any chance you ate at Family Home Cooking?" The expression on Margaret's face suggested she'd rather eat roadkill than dine at Family Home Cooking.

"We did," Griff answered.

"Jacqueline Culpepper works there. Both she and her youngest daughter."

I recalled our nasty spirited waitress and glanced down at the yearbook in my lap.

"She's changed a lot, ain't she?" A spiteful smile stretched across Margaret's face.

I snorted. Saying Jacqueline Culpepper had changed over the last thirty years was a gross understatement. Barely a shred of the woman who'd hugged her handsome husband and laughed in front of the Prom 1978 sign remained.

"Being married to Bobby John Culpepper couldn't have been easy. Susie might have been the first, but from what I heard she was far from the last." Margaret took the yearbook from me and held the book to her chest. "Do you think the Culpeppers killed my Susie?"

"All I can tell you for sure is Jacqueline Culpepper didn't mortally wound Susie in my vision." I took a deep breath. "She slapped her, twice."

Margaret flinched at the information. I glanced at Mysti, and she gave me a head shake. I nodded my understanding. I wouldn't say any more.

"I planned for us to go see the Culpeppers tomorrow." Griff turned off his tape recorder. "The address I have for them is 365 Ingram Street. Still correct?"

"They're still there." Margaret covered her mouth to yawn.

"We'll be getting out of your hair, ma'am." Mysti stood and grabbed my arm, giving me a hard jerk. "I apologize for Peri Jean disturbing you. She's new to this, and she gets excited."

"Don't apologize, please. This lets me know for sure

y'all are working on Susie's case. For the first time in a long time, I feel hope."

We said our goodbyes. I tried to get into the SUV with Griff, but Mysti beckoned me to ride with her. I plodded to her Toyota and got into the passenger side, priming myself for my slap on the wrist.

"I'm sorry, Mysti. I did the wrong thing."

"Whether you did or not, she loved it." Mysti pulled the car away from the curb, following Griff down the street. "The snow globe wasn't in the bag when we left Margaret's house. It wasn't there when I started getting ready to spend time with Griff. When did it get there? And how?"

"I can only guess Susie put it there."

"I don't understand how." Mysti muttered the words almost to herself. Then she turned to me. "You started giving Margaret details on the scuffle. I stopped you because the less she knows, the better. Now I want to know what you think. Did Jacqueline Culpepper kill Susie?"

"Not right then." The memory of the last words Jacqueline said to Susie came to me. I almost forgot them, getting yanked out of the vision so fast. "Jacqueline's child interrupted the fight, and she left. But as she was leaving she said something to Susie, and I read her lips."

"What was it?" Mysti cruised behind Griff's taillights, tapping her fingers on the steering wheel.

"'This isn't over.'"

Mysti pulled into the parking place I'd vacated what seemed like an eternity ago. She turned to me. "Bitch was right. It ain't over."

———

The Culpeppers lived a little way out of town. As soon as we turned onto Ingram Street, we passed a faded sign telling us we were entering Bonaventure Estates, a village of deed restricted ranchettes. The ranchettes consisted of oversized lots with cookie cutter brick ranch homes on them. Griff cruised down the narrow road, slowing nearly to a crawl at curves because there wasn't enough room for two vehicles to pass.

"I don't see house numbers." Mysti leaned forward, squinting at the houses.

"Bet this is them." I pointed several houses down where a sign reading "The Culpepper Team" graced the front yard.

Griff pulled into the driveway and parked behind a behemoth Ford pickup truck. He cut the engine and glanced first at me, then at Mysti.

"The Culpeppers don't want to meet with us, so be ready for anything."

"Are we dropping in on them?" I glanced around the yard, halfway expecting to see armed garden gnomes gearing up to run us off.

"Nope. I threatened to get a journalist friend of mine to revive the Susie Franklin story with special attention to her claims of inappropriate behavior from the coach." Griff's eyes gleamed like polished steel. I got the feeling he enjoyed this part of his job.

"You're ruthless." Mysti patted his arm and got out of

the SUV. I followed behind her, and Griff brought up the rear. This time Mysti knocked on the door.

Miss Meanypants from the diner, also known as Jacqueline Culpepper, answered. The lines around her mouth deepened.

"Reed Investigations." Mysti gave her a sugary smile. "I believe we have an appointment."

"It *would* be you three." Jacqueline held open the door and stepped aside to let us pass. Walking past her made my skin and muscles tighten as though expecting attack. "Go on into the living room. Bobby John's waiting in there."

I felt my eyes widen at the sight of Coach Bobby John Culpepper. The trim guy I saw in the yearbook picture from 1978 took up most of a full sized couch. He sat spraddle-legged, a big, red plastic glass clutched in one bloated hand. The slow, mysterious eyes hid in the folds of fat smothering his handsome features. Some folks aged well. Bobby John wasn't one of them.

"Y'all can sit on the hearth." Jacqueline flopped into a leather recliner, which protested with a squeal of un-oiled metal.

Mysti, Griff, and I crowded onto the requisite '80s cream and tan brick fireplace facade, squishing ourselves together so tight I smelled the dry spiciness of Griff's cigarillos.

"First thing I want to say is the three of you young people ought to be ashamed for threatening Mrs. Culpepper and myself in order to get us to speak to you." Bobby John rested his dark scowl on each of us in turn. "Susie Franklin's disappearance rocked this community, created a lot of sadness. Decent folk would let it fade into the past."

"Margaret Franklin hired us, sir." Griff opened his messenger bag and took out his recorder.

"No. Nuh-uh." Jacqueline leapt from her chair and pointed a finger at Griff like he was a little, yappy dog squatting to soil her ugly tan carpet. "We don't agree to having our statement recorded."

"Ma'am, neither I nor these two ladies are affiliated with official law enforcement. This is not a statement." Griff paused to let his words sink in. "This is nothing more than a conversation. Susie Franklin's mother wants some closure."

"The mother's as bad as the daughter, you ask me." Jacqueline Culpepper returned to her squeaky recliner and sat back down, staying near the edge of the seat, maybe in case she had to jump up and point her finger again.

"Now, sugar-lips, Margaret Franklin was taken in by Susie's lies. What if one of our kids came to you with a similar story?" Bobby John slurped out of his plastic cup and reached down beside the couch, grabbed a jumbo-sized bottle of generic brand soda and poured himself a refill.

"I'd have better sense than to believe it." Jacqueline crossed her arms over her chest.

"You would not," Bobby John shot back. Jacqueline waved off her husband and turned to us.

"You have to understand, Susie's accusations hurt us in the community. Bobby John almost lost his coaching job.

We had to take our oldest son out of preschool because the woman running it refused to let him come there." Her nostrils flared, and her eyes narrowed at the injustice. "It was an awful time."

"It was a sad time." Coach Bobby John contemplated his wife with a downturned mouth. "It disrupted a lot of good kids' senior year of high school, derailed the football program for the year, and took the focus off learning." He shook his head sadly. "The backlash from it hurt Susie Franklin so much. Despite what she said about me, I cared about her. She was a good student and a good athlete."

I had to hand it to Coach Bobby John. Had I not seen the vision in the snow globe, I might have believed the slimy toad. *Had Susie been lying?* All I really saw was Jacqueline acting inappropriately. From what I'd seen of her, the behavior could have been an everyday loss of reason.

"A lot of the girls had crushes on Coach Bobby John." Jacqueline glanced at her husband. "He's still handsome, but back then he was something else."

"I know you're telling the truth. I saw a picture of him in a yearbook from '78." I smiled at Coach Bobby John. He waved me off, chuckling, but sat up as straight as his bulk would allow.

Jacqueline glanced from me to her husband. Her cheeks flushed into red blotches, and her mouth curved into a sneer, which she aimed at me. The heat of her anger reached me from across the room. I turned my gaze to my feet. Did she actually think I was coming on to Coach Bobby John? I might make odd choices sometimes, but I never had a Jabba the Hutt fetish. Jacqueline's insecurity spoke louder than anything she said so far. A woman this jealous and worried either had reason to be that way or was completely neurotic. Which was it?

"I wish I'd never hired her to babysit." Jacqueline spoke the words the same way she might have sung a familiar song.

I raised my head to find her still glaring at me. This time I met her gaze and waited until she dropped hers.

"I think spending time here, among our things, seeing how happy me and Bobby John were together, made her start having fantasies." Lines appeared in the older woman's forehead as she spoke. "Then maybe she started thinking those fantasies were real."

"Susie's father died the year the poor girl started high school." Coach Bobby John shifted his bulk on the couch. The furniture's supports creaked as though they might give way. "Maybe she was looking for a father substitute."

Again, I took in Coach Bobby John's earnest expression, trying to rate the authenticity of the sympathy I saw on his face and heard in his voice. The way he reacted to my earlier compliment set off warning bells. Vain men loved an admiring audience. But had Coach Bobby John acted on his power? Then something else hit me. What happened between Bobby John and Susie thirty-five years ago only mattered if Bobby John made Susie disappear.

"I think we've lost sight of what Reed Investigations wants to discuss." I glanced at Griff. Boy, I hoped I wasn't shitting the bed. "We are not here to determine whether anything inappropriate went on between Coach Culpepper and Susie Franklin."

"Peri Jean is right." Griff bobbed his head. "At this point, it doesn't matter."

"But I never did anything," Bobby John said. I glanced at Jacqueline Culpepper just in time to see her roll her eyes. She caught me watching and shrank into the chair, digging her fingers into the armrests.

All doubt left me. He did it. No telling how many more teenage girls he screwed before he got too unattractive. His wife was, at the very least, mean and possibly unstable. These two could definitely have killed Susie Franklin. My head swam with the knowledge. I didn't realize I was rocking side to side until Mysti gripped my arm.

"Of course you did nothing." Griff frowned at me. "The real question here is whether either of you have any idea where Susie Franklin may have ended up or what happened to her."

"I never spoke to her again after the story broke." Jacqueline rubbed at one eye, shaking her head.

"Nor did I." Coach Bobby John kept his gaze trained on his wife.

"Bullshit." I spoke before I remembered I was working for Griff. I gave him a quick glance. It wouldn't do to get into a shouting match with Jacqueline. For one thing, she'd win. Even if she had to use the fire tools next to me to beat me into silence.

"Did you just call me a liar, baby?" Jacqueline's tone of voice sounded sweet, but murder burned behind her eyes.

I turned to Griff. He shrugged as if to say, *Might as well go ahead.*

"I know for a fact you went to see Susie Franklin after the story broke. You slapped her in the face."

Bobby John's head swiveled to regard his wife. His mouth dropped open. He must not have known.

"And where'd you get your information—what did your boss call you?—Peri Jean?" She put on a thick, hick accent to say my name.

"Mr. Reed didn't tell you what I do for him when he introduced me, did he?"

Jacqueline, sensing a falling shoe the way an animal senses danger, shook her head.

"I'm a medium. I talk to the dead."

"Oh, horse shit." Jacqueline shook her head.

"Horse shit won't help you, Mrs. Culpepper. I saw you come to Susie's house, scream at her, and slap her twice in the face." I glanced at her husband and saw a detail I could use. "Your wedding band matched the one Coach Culpepper is wearing. No telling how far it would have gone, but your little boy interrupted the two of you, crying. You left with him. Do you remember the last thing you said to Susie?"

The blood drained from Jacqueline's face, leaving it the color of chalk dust.

"You can't know what did or didn't happen so long ago. You'd have just been a baby."

"But I do know because I saw it, same as watching an old movie on TV." I locked gazes with the older woman, feeling like gunslingers must have felt waiting for the clock to strike high noon. "Do you want to tell Coach Culpepper what you said to Susie Franklin that day? Or would you like me to tell him for you?"

Jacqueline Culpepper sat in her recliner panting like a dog with the trots.

"Y'all are upsetting my wife," Bobby John said. "I want it to stop."

"Your wife told your teenage girlfriend, 'This isn't over.'" I raised my voice loud enough the neighbors probably heard it.

Coach Bobby John began to tremble. He swept his gaze over his wife, mouth moving silently.

"We saw her the day she went missing, okay?" Jacqueline Culpepper screamed.

"But, sugar-lips, we promised each other we'd never tell." Bobby John sounded like a toddler who'd been told to wait until his father got home. His words punched into me.

"I don't care. This weird bitch—"

I stood, not caring if I ended up going death match with Jacqueline. I'd fight her before I put up with her disrespect.

"Who you calling a bitch, you crazy bitch?"

Griff stood behind me and grabbed my arm.

"Don't." His breath was hot on my ear. "Get it under control. Now." He released me and faced the Culpeppers. "Tell me what you saw the day Susie disappeared. If you did nothing to her, you should have nothing to hide."

The Culpeppers glanced at each other. Jacqueline nodded at Bobby John.

"Mrs. Culpepper and myself had come from a meeting with the school board. We saw Susie Franklin walking near her home with Kevin Douglas."

"Kevin Douglas, you say?" Griff stepped forward to tower over Coach and Mrs. Culpepper. "Who is he?"

This must be pretty good if even Griff doesn't know about it. Nothing we'd uncovered seemed to surprise him until right then.

"Little freak was her boyfriend. Always going around wearing all black. Even dyed his hair." Bobby John waved one arm at his wife. "Go get the 1979 or the 1980 yearbook, sugar-lips."

Jacqueline marched from the room and went down the central hallway. Sounds of her rustling around came from one of the back bedrooms. She came back holding a 1979 yearbook, already open to the page she wanted to show us. Bobby John leaned forward to see what picture his wife had chosen. He nodded his approval.

"The yearbook staff always takes snapshots around campus to show the students in a less formal setting," he said.

The snapshot showed a kid wearing black slacks, a black suit jacket, and a black fedora hat. He stood next to Susie Franklin who wore her track outfit and was staring at someone out of the camera's frame. Judging by the longing expression on her face, I bet it was Coach Bobby John.

"Kevin Douglas quit school and left town right after Susie disappeared." Bobby John seemed to have recovered from his shock and snapped back into helpful citizen mode. "But he's back. He came back about a year ago."

Griff, Mysti, and I glanced at each other. Recently enough for him to be responsible for the most recent disappearance in the area.

"If anybody killed Susie Franklin, it's that kook." Jacqueline rose from her chair and walked to the front door and held it open.

It was time to hit and git, and we filed out silently. I bet we'd find somewhere else to eat supper when evening rolled around.

4

"What a pair of freaks." Griff started his SUV and backed slowly down the driveway and into the narrow county road. He drove a while and pulled over at a wide spot. He unbuckled his seatbelt and twisted to face me. "Peri Jean, you cannot work for me if you can't control your temper. Do we understand each other?"

I nodded, my cheeks on fire. Being sucked into a black hole would have been preferable to sitting there under Griff's stern glare.

"I'm sorry," I whispered and dropped my gaze to my cowboy boots.

Griff pulled back onto the road and started driving again. "Any insights from either of you?"

"Other than Coach Bobby John is a fantastic liar?" I longed to light up a cigarette but didn't quite dare do it in Griff's spiffy ride. If he didn't smoke in here, he sure as hell didn't want me doing it.

"Any serious ones?" Griff glanced at me in the rearview mirror. I cringed.

"Jacqueline could have killed Susie in a rage. Bobby John would have helped her dispose of the body." I swallowed hard, waiting for the next rebuke.

Neither Mysti nor Griff said anything for several long moments. I started to think they disagreed.

"They definitely have an unhealthy relationship." Mysti loosened her seatbelt and half turned in the seat. "I can't imagine where and how they'd have done the killing."

"Snatch Susie off the street. Kill her in the car." Griff turned onto the highway and drove toward Nazareth. "Strangulation wouldn't have made a mess. As for body disposal, look at this place. There's secluded burial sites everywhere you turn."

"This Kevin Douglas character could have done the same thing," Mysti said.

"If he even exists." Griff pulled into the motel parking lot and parked in front of his room. "I can't believe I never heard of him before we talked to the Culpeppers." He pulled the keys out of the ignition. "I'll need to do some online research on him before we barge into his life. Y'all up for a working lunch in motel hell?" He pulled a fold of bills from his pocket and held them out to Mysti. "On me."

Mysti and I found the vending machine tucked into an alley next to the laundry room. The odor of bleach and hot fabric competed with the mildewy scent of permanently damp concrete. A mosquito lit on my arm as soon as I stopped moving. I swatted it away but another took its place. Mysti handed me a couple of the dollar bills Griff gave her. The vending machine had no bottled water, so I chose an orange soda and a bag of cheese flavored tortilla chips.

"I screwed up with Griff." I wanted reassurance I hadn't blown my chance.

"Not too bad." Mysti put in her money and chose two different kinds of soft drinks and chips. "Griff is about getting the job done, and you got results. So that counts in your favor. But you need to watch yourself."

We walked back to Griff's room. Mysti raised her hand to knock but turned to me. "What about the snow globe? I didn't think about telling you to bring it to the Culpeppers. Why don't you go get it? Susie seems to prefer communicating with you through it."

I let myself back into the room I was ostensibly sharing with Mysti, grabbed the globe, and went back to Griff's room.

Griff and Mysti sat at the tiny table drinking their soft drinks and eating their chips.

"You find anything out about Kevin Douglas on the Internet?"

"Motel's Wi-Fi is a joke. I'll have to use my Internet anywhere card." Griff ate another chip and made a face. "And these are stale." He began typing on his laptop.

I set the snow globe on the nightstand and stared at it while I forced down the rest of my stale chips. The bed shifted as Mysti sat down next to me. I picked up the globe, shook it, and sat it back down. Together we watched the fake snow drift down and settle on the stylized skyline of Reno.

The sound of keys clicking on the keyboard stopped. "See anything?"

"Nothing," I turned to Mysti. "You?"

She shook her head at me and spoke to Griff. "What about you? Any luck?"

"Kevin Douglas has never been arrested and doesn't have a mortgage or a car loan. His worst sin is bad credit." He closed the laptop. "I got his address. It's out the same way the Culpeppers lived. Y'all want to drop in for supper?"

"If the other choice is the vending machine, yes." Mysti stood and brushed chip crumbs off her skirt.

"Sweetie, I'm willing to take you back to Family Home Cooking." He winked at me. "Me and Peri Jean'll wait for you in the parking lot."

"I'll be right there to collect you when they throw you out." I took a sip of the syrupy orange soda.

"Cowards, both of you." Mysti swung her handbag at my legs.

Griff made a chicken sound at her and pushed back his chair. He stood, stretching with his arms over his head until his bones popped. "Let's go make Kevin Douglas's acquaintance."

I grabbed the snow globe, and we left in the SUV. Griff turned in his seat and fastened his gaze on the globe. I waited for him to tell me what a dumb idea it was to bring it along.

"Don't get it out until I signal," he said. "I've got an idea."

On the drive to wherever Kevin Douglas lived, I replayed highlights of my relationship with Dean Turgeau, comparing his reactions to my otherworldliness to Griff's. Different world. As always, I ended my thoughts scolding myself for even trying with Dean. I should have seen the writing on the wall with him. Next time—if I let there be a next time—I would be smarter. Not let my heart get broken into a zillion sharp bits.

The monotone voice on Griff's GPS took us back out into the wilds surrounding Nazareth. This time, there was no sign welcoming us to a deed restricted community. The first domicile we passed appeared to be a stucco house of some size until we passed it, and I noticed a mobile home attached to the stucco facade. Griff slowed the SUV to a crawl.

"We're looking for 643," he said.

Several mobile homes down, a group sat in the front yard in lawn chairs, a cooler of beer on the grass in front of them. An older man wearing full cowboy regalia, except for his leather house shoes, hurried down to his mailbox to meet us, flagging us down by waving one arm in a chopping motion.

"Who y'all looking for?" Cowboy had short black stumps for teeth and didn't mind showing them off.

"Kevin Douglas," Griff said.

This answer confused Cowboy, and he stared at Griff, his mouth hanging open.

"Get out of the damn way, you idiot," said a voice

behind Cowboy. A pudgy hand shoved the skinny old man away. A guy about my age took his place.

"Whoever you people came out here to find ain't here. Why don't you turn your yuppie mobile around and go back the way you came?"

Griff sighed and dug in his pocket, fishing out a twenty and palming it. When he spoke I barely recognized his voice. "Listen, brah, I ain't the po-lice, and I ain't here for trouble. What I am here for is to talk to Kevin Douglas. Now you either gonna move your ass out my way and let me go on looking for him, or you gonna tell me where he is." He flashed the twenty at the guy. "Now I'm willing to give you a little gratuity for the information, but I ain't gonna fuck around with you."

Griff had his back to me, so I couldn't see his face. Whatever the pudgy guy saw there made him take a step back and shuffle on his feet.

"It's five more houses down. Double-wide painted tan. Got a white van out front." He held his hand out for the twenty, and Griff passed it to him.

We drove on, finding the house with no problem. Kevin Douglas met us at the door. Pudge or Cowboy must have called and warned him.

"Let me talk first." Griff got out of the SUV. Mysti and I followed and stood behind him.

"Can I he'p you folks?" Kevin wore a threadbare pearl snap cowboy shirt, blue jeans, and rubber flip-flops. He had a dish towel slung over his shoulder. He reached up to rub the patchy beard covering his face.

"I'm Griffin Reed of Reed Investigations." Griff handed

him a card. "Margaret Franklin hired me to look into the disappearance of her daughter. We were told the two of you were friends."

Kevin's gaze dulled, and he dropped his hand from his face and held open the door. "C'mon in."

We followed Kevin through the living room and into a small dining room off the kitchen. Our host gestured at a rickety glass-topped table.

"Y'all want a beer?"

Mysti and I shook our heads.

"I'll take one," Griff said.

We all sat down. My chair rocked to one side, worrying me it might collapse in a heap of cheap metal and bamboo. I leaned my shoulder against one thin wall, the kind common to mobile homes, papered with a pattern designed to look outdated long before the owners made the final payment.

Kevin came from the kitchen carrying two cans of Milwaukee's cheapest. He clunked one down in front of Griff and opened the other. "I'm sorry about those stupid tweakers hassling you. They think they're a badass operation. Really just a bunch of clowns."

"Seems like they're everywhere." Griff took a pull off his beer and somehow managed not to shudder.

"They's here when I moved back home last year. Wouldn't have come back, period, but Daddy had a stroke, and I ain't got the heart to stow him in a nursing home." He opened his beer and drank most of it in one swallow.

"When did you move away from Nazareth?" Griff sipped his beer again and set it carefully on the table.

"Not long after Susie disappeared. Now why don't you tell me who sent you out here. Margaret?"

"It wasn't her," Griff said.

"Then it was the Culpeppers." He rubbed his beard again, nodding. "Yep. They's real upset when I showed back up. Told me I's never supposed to come back here." He killed his beer and set the can aside.

"Why were they so determined to have you out of town?" The words came out before I remembered Griff said to let him do the talking. He shot me a look, and I shrugged in apology.

"What'd the Culpeppers tell y'all?" Kevin sat very still.

"That you and they were the last three people to see Susie Franklin alive." Griff stared at Kevin until he pushed himself out of his chair and walked into the kitchen. The sucking sound of a refrigerator opening drifted back out to us. Kevin came back sipping on his new beer and sat back down.

"I 'spect we were." Kevin squinted at the wall. "You know, it all happened so long ago, I don't even remember what Susie looked like. All I remember is what a good friend she was."

Griff dug in his messenger bag and took out a copy of one of Susie's pictures. Kevin, holding his beer in both hands, leaned forward, staring at the picture, the same far-off expression on his face.

"Yep. There she is. Boy, I had an awful crush on her." He reached out to nudge Griff. "You 'member them high school crushes on a girl you knew you'd never have? But you couldn't quit hanging out with her and hoping? That's how it was with Susie. She was too sweet to tell me to get lost, so there I was."

"I bet it burned when Susie took up with Coach Culpepper." Griff took another sip of his beer, his throat working to make it go down and stay there.

"Yeah, but it was one of those things where you know it ain't going to work out. I mean, what's he gonna do? Kick his wife out and move Susie in?" He killed the second beer and went to get a third, his steps unsteady. He flopped back into his chair. For an awful moment it looked like it was going to dump him onto the ratty maroon carpet. "For a long time, I thought she's blowing smoke. Lying, you know." He raised shaggy eyebrows at Mysti and me to bring home his meaning. I nodded.

"You still think it was her imagination?" I had a good idea it wasn't, but I wanted to hear what Kevin would say. Griff shot me another look. I rounded my shoulders.

Kevin's face turned a dull red, and he stared at the beer in his hands. "I think I'd still believe it if I hadn't followed 'em one day." He chuckled, not even able to look at us. "Can't believe I did it. Followed 'em out to the old rest area. They walked into those woods, pulled down their pants, and did what people do."

Judging by the look on his face, Kevin stayed for the whole show.

"And you stayed friends with Susie afterward?" This time Mysti spoke up, earning her own glare from Griff.

"It pissed me off, if that's what you're asking. I ignored her for about a month. Then she called me boo-hooing because she'd missed her period."

"Did Culpepper know about the pregnancy?" Griff spoke quickly, probably trying to beat Mysti or me to the punch.

"Oooh, yeah. Pretty much ended their little romance."

"What happened?" I asked. "I mean, was it a big ugly scene?"

"I went with her to his office one day during football practice. He blew a fuse. Threw some money at her and told her to get rid of it." Kevin ran his tongue over his lower lip, squinting at the wall behind me. "It was me who took her to the clinic in Dallas. Had to cough up extra money because Coach was cheap. And it was me who took the reaming on using condoms from one of the nurses." His lips twisted into an unhappy smile. "Y'all know what's funny 'bout the whole thing?"

Griff shook his head. I didn't move. None of it was funny to me.

"Poor little Susie was a like a dog whose owner kicks it from day one. She went through the abortion, came back to town, and started mooning after him." Kevin picked up his empty beer can but didn't bother to get up for another. "'Course the Coach had enough sense to be scared off by then. She was so hurt. Saddest thing I ever seen."

I hurt for Susie, deep in my chest where all my failed relationships hid out. I was a grown woman and still expected things to work like they do in romance novels. A girl not even out of high school would have gagged on such a bitter taste of heartbreak.

"You think she broke the story to get back at Culpepper?" Griff frowned at the table.

"It's real possible." Kevin stood and put one hand on the table to steady himself. "Going for another beer. You want one?"

Griff shook his head. "You have any idea where Susie might've gone?"

"She told me she was running away and that she'd write once she got where she was going." He sat back down, never having gone for his new beer. "Never did. About a month after she disappeared, it got around town Margaret hired a private detective. Culpepper cornered me at school. Said he'd tell about seeing me with Susie the day she disappeared if I didn't get out of town. Laid into me pretty good."

"You mean he beat you?" Mysti's nose wrinkled.

"Yep." Kevin pushed back his graying hair and showed us a deep scar on his forehead. "The ring he used to wear back then—probably too fat for it now—caught me just right." He left the table to get another beer, swaying on his feet and holding onto the cabinets.

Griff leaned close to me and whispered, "The snow globe."

I took it out of my bag and handed it to him. By the time Kevin came back, Griff had it sitting on the table at his place.

"Aw, Susie loved this thing." He picked it up, smiling, and turned it over to make the snow swirl.

Griff nudged me and gestured to Kevin. I watched the globe carefully but saw no sign of movement inside it. I shook my head at Griff. He deflated and sat immobile while Kevin upended the globe and stared into it.

"Funniest thing." Kevin spoke to the snow globe. "Got the feeling that last time I talked to Susie, she'd moved on from Culpepper, met somebody new."

"Why's that?" Griff sat straighter.

"Intuition, I guess. She didn't mention Coach once, but she had that same glow about her she had when him and her was together."

Griff questioned Kevin several more times but got nothing more out of him.

Ten minutes later, we sat in the SUV in Kevin Douglas's yard. I don't know how Griff or Mysti felt, but I felt like I'd committed the losing error of a baseball game. I held the globe on my lap, moving it back and forth between my hands. The black opal flared to life on my chest, and white light glowed from the globe.

"She's here." I might have said more, but the vision took over my conscious. Then I was again looking at the world from inside Susie Franklin's body. Susie and I trod through the weeds on the side of a two-lane road, which stretched off into the foreseeable distance. The coming night had stained the wide open sky a blurry purple color and whatever heat the day held had begun its retreat. Susie shivered and pulled her coat around her. Her apprehension seeped into my emotions. I wished I could tell her to go back home. Nothing but bad stuff awaited her.

The sound of a car coming toward us fast filled our ears. Susie turned and peered into the deepening dusk and smiled, her body relaxing with relief. The car appeared on the horizon, its headlights almost blinding. The driver slowed to a stop on the deserted highway right alongside Susie.

Fear of something I didn't want to see blossomed in me, but I forced myself to stay with Susie. I might see who picked her up.

I tried to look for details on the car, but Susie's attention was focused on the window. Because I was inside her body, mine was too. She leaned down to peer into the passenger window, her heart picking up speed. A blurry figure leaned across the seat and rolled down the window. His words were warped with the passage of time and my inability to access that part of the spirit world.

Susie's feelings, however, told me a lot. No longer was she afraid. Susie felt relieved to see this person. She got into his car, pulling her duffle bag into her lap. I saw the top of the snow globe peeking out.

I came back to myself to see Griff had us halfway back to town. Mysti turned to him.

"Peri Jean's okay. You can slow down."

The noise of the SUV's engine eased, and the passing landscape slowed.

"I'm sorry." My mouth felt thick and full of fur, as though I'd woken from a deep sleep. "Did I scare y'all?"

"Your eyes rolled back. Griff got a little upset." Mysti patted my leg and handed me a bottle of water. "I told him you'd be fine."

"You don't do anything like that, Mysti." Griff's voice had a tight, defensive edge to it. "You were just gone, Peri Jean. Scared the hell out of me." His forced laugh sounded like bones rattling on a dark night. "At least tell me you saw something pretty good in exchange for giving me a few more gray hairs."

"I think I did."

Griff pulled into the parking lot of a convenience store and turned off the SUV's engine. He unbuckled his seatbelt and turned to face me.

"Take a drink of water, and then tell me what you saw."

I did as he asked, going through the whole vision. "My two takeaways? She took the snow globe with her when she ran away, and she knew the person who picked her up."

"No ideas where he took her?" Griff took out his cellphone and began tapping in notes.

I shook my head.

"No ideas where he picked her up?"

I thought about it, going back over my memory of the surroundings several times. "Not really. The highway had two lanes and was sort of deserted."

"This is still a breakthrough," Griff said. "I'd like you to continue trying to contact her."

He went inside the convenience store and came back out with a couple of boxes of fried chicken and a bag of drinks. We took it back to the motel and ate in the room Mysti and I were sharing. Or not sharing, as it happened. Griff and she retired to his room soon after we finished eating. I listened to the headboard bang on the wall as I sat staring at the snow globe and trying to think of a surefire way to contact Susie.

When Mysti took me on as her student, she showed me several traditional ways mediums contacted the spirit world. I set the snow globe on the table in front of me with the track shirt on one side and Susie's picture on the other. I focused myself, shutting off the chatter of my mind, and concentrated on the items. I went deep inside myself and called for Susie.

At first nothing happened. I kept up my efforts, the intense concentration draining my energy. The snow in the snow globe began to swirl again. This time, instead of lighting up, it darkened. The cartoonish letters spelling Reno were replaced by a familiar setup I couldn't quite place.

A wide driveway branched off into parking spaces in front of a white brick building. Next to the building, metal squares dotted the impossibly green lawn. I waited to get pulled into Susie's body, but I stayed where I was, looking over the whole scene at one time.

A car came up the driveway and pulled into one of the parking spaces. It was an old Ford, probably a model from the 1940s. The car was beat all to hell with one red door, one black door, and a mashed in front fender. The car sat there, engine ticking as it cooled. Was this the car Susie got into? I didn't know. The other vision didn't give me this kind of overview.

The car's driver door popped open, and a young guy wearing blue jeans and a plaid pearl snap shirt got out. He went around to the back door and opened it, leaning inside, gathering up a bundle. It must have been heavy because he bent his legs, straining to lift his burden, and took two staggering steps backward.

I noticed the shock of Susie Franklin's white-blond hair

before I saw anything else. Her head lolled on the guy's arm as he carried her inside. I stared at his face and saw nothing familiar. All I knew for sure was he wasn't Kevin Douglas.

The vision ended as fast if someone had turned off a TV. I sat at the small table breathing hard, my sweat growing cold. The greasy chicken congealed into a nauseous lump in my stomach. The shakes started and came so hard and fast I slammed my knee into the table's leg. The pain broke me out of my fit, and I tried to force myself under control, grabbing the sides of the table with both hands and clenching my body as tight as I could. Little by little, the panic lessened its hold on me. I closed my eyes and leaned back in the chair and stared at the ceiling.

I was pretty sure the last vision took place at the rest stop Mysti and I passed on the way into Nazareth. I thought I remembered Griff saying it had been a crime scene in the disappearances to which he wanted to connect Susie's disappearance. All of a sudden, I knew I had to go out there. If I ever wanted to find out what happened to Susie, the rest stop would have the answers. I grabbed the snow globe, Susie's school photo, and the track shirt and shoved them all into my bag. Then I grabbed Mysti's car keys again.

My cellphone buzzed with a text message.

I felt the magic all the way in here, Mysti wrote. *Give us a few minutes, and we'll join you.*

I paced on the walkway outside the row of motel rooms, getting antsier by the moment. It felt like something was pulling me, begging me to get in the car and go out to the rest area by myself. Unable to help myself, I took a few steps toward Mysti's Toyota but stopped. *I'm smarter than this.* The urge came again to go, go, go. This time, I distanced myself from it and tried to identify where it came from. It was gone as though it had never been.

Griff and Mysti came out of his motel room. He held a shotgun in one hand. "You can't be too safe."

Mysti took one look at me and stopped short. "What is it? Your skin's the color of Elmer's glue, and you're sweating."

The itch to leave came again, this time whispering for me to take the shotgun from Griff and leave him and Mysti behind. Now I knew the thoughts didn't come from me. I'd never try something so foolish.

Mysti raised her head to stare at the sky and turned in a slow circle, her chest rising and falling faster by the second. "Something's trying to pull you out there."

"You feel it too?" My relief made me take a step toward my mentor, seeking the comfort of her confidence.

"I've never felt anything like it." Mysti continued staring at the sky as though waiting for the next wave to hit. "If all the people who disappeared felt that, they didn't stand a chance."

"Let's go see who or what wants the pleasure of our company." Griff used his key fob to unlock the SUV, and we piled in.

———

A FULL MOON HUNG OVERHEAD, its cool light silhouetting deer standing along the roadside. Most of them whirled to run from Griff's SUV. They jumped over the barbed wire fences as though they had oiled springs in their hind legs and kept running until the darkness swallowed them.

"I remember the rest area being somewhere right around here." Griff let off the gas. "Either of you see it? Wasn't there a sign?"

"There." Mysti pointed to a driveway with a chain stretched across it.

Griff pulled up to the chain. "I've got bolt cutters."

"It's private property," I said. "Let's climb over."

I expected an argument from Griff or Mysti but didn't get one. The chain was too high for me to step over, so I ducked under, childhood memories of playing limbo flitting through my mind. I held Griff's shotgun while he helped Mysti navigate the chain. Together we walked down the long narrow driveway toward two narrow buildings, presumably restrooms, set amid a scattering of covered picnic tables.

I took out the small flashlight I carried in my bag and shone it around. From the looks of it, the chain didn't keep too many people out. Broken brown glass, probably from beer bottles, carpeted the asphalt lot. Rotting paper rested on the picnic tables. Some scholar had spray painted a pentagram on the side of the restroom with the words "The Devil Lives Here" next to it.

Griff took out his own flashlight and shined it across the words. "Found a message board online where a bunch of people claim the missing people were killed here at the rest stop. Folks say it's haunted by their souls. Supposedly the restrooms are full of graffiti too."

"Did anybody find proof a crime took place here?" I stood back from the building, knowing I'd have to go in at some point but wanting to put it off as long as possible. It was easy to understand why people thought this place haunted. A low hum of something nasty came off it. Though I couldn't see any spirits walking, I felt something not right in the air, in the ground, in the very molecules of this place.

"If so, it's not public." Griff took a few steps toward the squat building housing the restrooms and glanced back at Mysti and me. Mysti hung back, her arms crossed over her chest. She stared at the building the way I'd stare at a coiled-up rattlesnake. Noticing both Griff and me watching her, she moved forward, her lips set in a determined line. I caught her arm.

"I'll go in. Susie may not even contact me again tonight. You stay here in case something goes wrong."

"You're shaking, and you're going to let me stay out here?" She choked out a short laugh. "What kind of mentor would I be if I didn't go with you?"

"I'm going in first." Griff walked ahead of us. "Might be someone dangerous in there."

Normally, I'd have marched in right alongside him, but the closer I got to the building, the worse I felt. Nausea and dizziness scuba dived in my head. My footsteps felt too light, as though I might float away.

Griff reached the door and turned back to me. "Did you see which side Susie was carried into?"

I sorted through my memory and took a few steps backward to recreate the scene in my mind. I raised one arm and pointed to my left.

"Women's." Griff kicked open the door and went inside, making as much noise as he could. The light from his flashlight flashed in the high narrow windows. Several times, he yelled, "Anybody in here?" He came back out. "It's clear. One stall door is jammed closed, but nobody's in the stall."

I turned to Mysti. Together we took a deep breath. I cleared my mind as she'd taught me and thought about Susie. Maybe she would show up and give me some answers before I had to spend too much more time in this little pocket of hell. We walked toward the open door. Griff stood aside to let us pass and handed Mysti his flashlight. She shone her light on the wall with the stalls, and I turned my light on the row of sinks set under the windows.

Grim streaks of black mildew smeared the tile walls. Three of the four sinks had no faucets. The basins bore the same dark stains as the ones covering the walls. The fourth basin contained some sort of nest made of twigs and scraps of garbage. I didn't want to meet whatever called it home. Cold sweat ran down my back, and my mouth took on the texture of sandpaper. The dizziness swirling in my head turned to a steady hum I felt in my back teeth. My stomach heaved and rocked as my body tried to adjust. I turned my flashlight on the stalls.

Of the four toilet stalls, one had a door. Judging by what I could see in the bowls of the other three toilets, I knew I didn't want to know what sanitation horror lurked behind door number four.

"Susie?" I dug in my bag for the snow globe and took it out. Mysti turned her flashlight on it. The globe was dark and still. The heaviness of this place blanketed me, darkening the gloom, pushing me down. Something moved against the back wall of the restroom. Mysti let out a sharp scream. I jumped and had to juggle the snow globe to keep from dropping it. I crept toward the sound.

"Peri Jean, don't." Mysti's voice trembled with an edge of high panic. This was the first time I ever heard her sound truly scared. I was a few steps away from where I thought I'd heard the sound and kept going. I'd instigated this whole trip. My pride couldn't stand it all being for nothing. Not with Griff watching and a possible semi-regular paying gig riding on it. It didn't matter how this place made me feel.

I shone my flashlight on the filthy wall, running it over where someone had written "He is watching you" in red paint. At least I hoped it was red paint. Odd thing was, it looked wet. I shoved the snow globe under the arm holding the flashlight and reached out to touch it.

"Peri Jean, no," Mysti screamed. Her running footsteps pounded behind me, but she never got there. Or maybe she did, and I had disappeared. Her shouts came from far away. She yelled for Griff to help her, to do something. I turned back around to face them and found the restroom empty. Bright overhead lights beamed down on me, and the white tile sparkled around me. I turned off the flashlight, shoved it into my back pocket, and turned back to the wall and touched the spot where I'd seen the writing.

The writing was still there, but had changed to it "He's here." I touched it, and my hand left a red smear on the clean tile.

Every muscle, every nerve in my body sang soprano, and my skin tightened. I turned a slow circle, expecting someone to be waiting behind me, but I had the bathroom to myself. It was past time to get out. Faintly, very faintly, I heard Mysti and Griff calling my name.

"I'm here," I yelled back as loud as I could, walking around the bathroom in search of a spot where they seemed close. The formerly dilapidated bathroom was so clean I actually smelled bleach and hand soap. The only similarity it shared with the place I entered with Griff and Mysti was that one stall door was closed while the other three hung open.

"Peri Jean?" Mysti sounded farther away than ever. "Are you okay?"

"I think so. I'm right here." The black opal around my neck flashed with power. I touched it, hoping it would beam me back to Griff and Mysti. It shot magic into my fingertips, but I stayed where I was. Wild, electric fear buzzed at the edge of my brain. I needed to get out before it got the better of me and I lost control. "Can you hear me?"

Nobody answered. The world had gone silent other than the hum of the electric lights. This had to be a vision, and there had to be a way to exit it. Maybe Susie wanted me to see something in the snow globe. I held it up and saw the water inside had gone blood red.

"Ugh." Revulsion overrode my good sense, and I raised the snow globe to throw it. At the last second, I thought better of it and set it down near my feet.

I glanced at the door where I came in and had an idea. Taking deep breaths and trying to keep the hysteria bubbling inside me at bay, I walked toward the door and reached for the handle. My hand hit an invisible field, causing iridescent ripples of color to flash, and stopped an inch or so from the handle. I pushed harder. The color ripples dimpled but stopped my progress. I was trapped.

The horror I'd been trying so hard to contain exploded. I slammed my body at the door and hit the same wall of resistance. It threw me backward and dumped me on my ass in the middle of the tile floor. I gained my feet and repeated the exercise, with the same results. I saw the snow globe out of the corner of my eye and went to pick it up again. The red water was gone. Inside the snow globe was a miniature of the restroom in which I was trapped. A curled figure lay on the floor, blood spreading around it. I recognized my purple blouse and tan cowboy boots. I batted the thing away from me. It slid across the floor and came to rest underneath the row of sinks.

It was then I heard the sound. It was a shuffling, secretive sound, like feet sliding on a gritty floor. Another thumping, pattering sound accompanied it. Maybe I'd been hearing it the whole time I lost my shit; maybe it had recently started. I didn't know. All I knew was the sound came from the fourth stall, the one with the closed door.

Every instinct screamed at me to run, but there was nowhere to go. I stood paralyzed, the black opal heating to a burning lump on my chest. The tiny sounds of locusts humming and branches rubbing together outside drifted into the room. They echoed off the walls and floors, louder in the reverent silence than they had any business being. I finally got one foot to move, but it was in the wrong direction, away from the parking lot. Instead, I took one step after another to the closed bathroom stall, unable to stop, barely able to breathe through the apprehension clogging my throat.

The door swung open as I approached, whining on its hinges. The stall's occupant raised her head to stare at me through darkened, hollow eye sockets.

A scream—not my own—ripped through my head. I felt strong hands around my neck and a knee digging into my stomach. The hands relaxed, and the person crawled off me.

I snapped myself back into the bathroom and the horror suspended over the toilet in front of me. I recognized the shock of blond hair. Susie Franklin. Wild and painful prickles danced underneath my skin, flooding my bloodstream with spikes of energy. Still, I couldn't move. Some force held me in thrall.

Susie had been suspended over the toilet with a chain that ran out of one of the vent windows high in the wall. Her killer had taken her eyes and hollowed out her chest. Her hand held a broken strand of beads. One by one, the beads slid off the strand with maddening slowness, plummeting to the floor where they disappeared in an iridescent ripple.

The layer between this place and the real one, my mind supplied.

Whistling came from outside the building, some tune I didn't recognize. Footsteps crunching on the asphalt. I was no longer alone. *He's here.*

The chain suspending the woman tightened. It groaned against the window sill. The corpse in front of me swayed, her feet sliding on the dirty floor. This was the furtive sound I'd heard two lifetimes ago, when I was still innocent of the abomination before me. The whistling continued throughout it all. The corpse stopped moving. Hollow footsteps sounded outside the building, a metronome to the whistled tune.

He's coming. I've got to run. Whoever did this, whoever hurt Susie Franklin is coming inside this bathroom. Even if everything I'm seeing and hearing is an echo of the past, I'm in it. He might be able to do something to me. But where do I run?

The door swung open, and I backed against the wall. Someone came into the bathroom with me. There was no way for me to tell if he was the same man I saw carry Susie into the restroom because he wore a hollowed out animal head as a mask. The horrible thing might have started out as a horse, but great care had been taken to replace the horse's ears with rabbit ears. Deer horns had been affixed to the top of the animal's head. The snout was open, displaying boar's tusks.

My visitor held aloft a long knife with a hook—the kind hunters used to gut their kills—set into the blade. The knife had red smears on it. The hands wrapped around its handle were bloodstained, their cuticles colored black with blood. But the knife was nothing compared to what I saw when I raised my eyes to the killer's face. What I saw helped me find my voice, and a scream I didn't know I had in me pealed out of my mouth, abrading my throat with its force.

It was the absolute void of nothing in the killer's dull eyes. It nearly drove me mad with terror.

My chest tightened, and my heart throbbed. My vision wavered. Time stood still. My mind tried to shut down from the fear. If I didn't get myself under control, I wouldn't be able to help myself, and I had to help myself because there was nobody else to help me.

The man in front of me cocked his head to one side like a dog trying to understand what his human master is saying. The corners of his dead eyes crinkled. *Is he smiling at me? Oh no, I think he is.* I screamed because there wasn't another damn thing I could do.

Somewhere distant, Mysti's voice came to me. She chanted the words, "Bring her back. Bring her back where she belongs. This is her time and her place. Separate her from where she does not belong."

The black opal burned at my chest, its magic causing my adrenaline to spike even harder. I rocked on my feet and reached out a hand to steady myself.

"Mmmm-mmm. Ain't you something special. Just what I been waiting for," said the man with the abomination on his head. His hand tightened around his knife. He raised it head high and sprang at me. I danced away and brought my knee up, aiming for his family jewels. We never connected. The iridescent wave, which kept me from grabbing the door to the parking lot, appeared between us.

"Guardian of the light, protect Peri Jean Mace. Bring Peri Jean Mace back to the place where she belongs." Mysti's voice reverberated both within and without my body. I shook with the force of it. A crack appeared in the corner of the room, letting in blinding light and the smell of fresh air.

The killer, following my gaze, let out a low, rumbling growl at what he saw. The crack widened a tiny bit. He turned his attention back to me, his stare like a hot probe on my skin.

Please, please just a little bit more. I crept toward the opening, twisting often to make sure the bad man wasn't right behind me. When I got close enough, I reached for the crack's edge and tugged, trying to pull it wider. The crack at the top extended nearly to the ceiling. I pulled and prayed, doing everything I could to make it wide enough so I could get back to Mysti and Griff.

"Periiiiii Jeeeeaaaan." The bad man's whisper shook the whole world.

I faced him and pressed my back against the wall near the crack. Icy sweat ran down my body, and I began to shake.

The bad man reached behind him and pulled out the snow globe. He shook it at me, making the fake snow inside float and swirl. "There's no escape, Peri Jean Mace."

He bent his knees and leapt at me. I screamed and held my hands out to ward him off. He hit the membrane and dissipated into a million little colored dots. The black opal sent painful shocks into my skin. Had it made him disappear? I didn't think so. The killer seemed to know exactly how to operate in this place. He was playing with me.

The black opal heated again. The shiny clean bathroom began to fade, the nasty old bathroom visible behind a dull film. Mysti and Griff charged toward me, blurry and hazy, and still not quite with me.

"You see her?" Mysti screamed. "Grab her. Pull her."

Griff snatched one arm and Mysti got the other. They jerked at me, their faces contorting with effort. I tried to come toward them, but something held me fast. I turned to see what it was, and the man wearing the horse head had my legs. I kicked at him, sobbing.

"Banish the one who does evil." Mysti let go of me and reached into the pocket of her skirt. She came out with her hand cupped and threw the contents at my captor. I fell into Griff, who staggered backward with my weight. We tumbled onto the floor together.

"You okay?" He said the words between gasps.

I tried to speak but couldn't do more than wheeze. I gripped Griff's arm in thanks, and he nodded his understanding, still panting from the effort. I began to brush whatever Mysti had thrown from me. It had a gritty texture and stuck to my clammy hands.

"What is this shit?" I wiped my hands on my jeans and left behind tiny white specks.

"Blessed salt." Mysti threw her arms around me and held me so tight I felt her heart drumming in her chest. She pushed away from me and stared into my face. "Are you okay? What happened? Was he a ghost?"

"I'll answer all your questions on one condition," I said.

"What?"

"We get the fuck out of this piss palace."

"Not a problem." Griff got to his feet and pulled me up with him. We lit out of the bathroom as fast as we could. The sky outside was light with dawn. I stopped to stare at it, my mouth hanging open. It couldn't have been later than one in the morning when we rolled up to the rest stop. Where had the hours gone?

5

Griff and Mysti bundled me into the SUV. Griff got a blanket from the cargo area and spread it over me. I realized I was shaking head to toe and reached for it, pulling it up to my neck. I curled into a ball on the seat, leaned my head on the window, and watched Griff and Mysti go back into the restroom. They came out carrying armloads of candles, Mysti's athame, and vials of mystery substances. They schlepped their bundles around the side of the SUV. Dimly, I heard the cargo doors open, heard their voices as they deposited their loads, but it seemed as though they were distant, like characters on TV.

Griff and Mysti climbed into the front of the SUV. The engine started, and we went backward.

"You ready to tell us what you saw in there?" Griff's voice floated back to me.

The words wouldn't come. I didn't want to do anything

other than lay there in my blanket, watching the scenery roll past.

"Leave her be." Mysti dug in her bag and came out with a piece of wax paper twisted on both ends. "I think she's slipping into shock. Get us out of here, and I'll take care of her." Mysti unbuckled her seat belt and climbed into the back with me. She pushed the piece of wax paper at me. I ignored it.

"Don't make me force this into you." Her voice carried a note of determination. "It's my special remedy for shock, and it's going to help you feel better."

"Let's get out of Nazareth." Griff drove down the road that brought us into this crazy place. "We'll take a few hours off."

Mysti pushed the wax paper at me, and I turned my face away from her. She sighed.

"Peri Jean? Take Mysti's remedy." Griff made his voice sound cheerful, as though nothing was wrong. "It'll help. I promise."

Mysti shoved the remedy at me again. I wanted to try it because I felt awful, but I couldn't quite get my hand to reach for it. Mysti unfolded the paper, revealing a black, sticky substance.

"Lick it. You'll like the taste. It's sweet. I use tamarind as the base."

I reached for it, hand shaking so hard I could barely control it. Mysti took my fingers and closed them on the wax paper. I pushed it at my mouth, barely parting my lips in time. The oily sweetness of tamarind coated my tongue.

I forced myself to swallow. Mysti pushed a water bottle to my lips, and I drank.

"There. Give it a few minutes." She sat back next to me.

I closed my eyes against the world, unable to do anything else. Within a few seconds, Mysti's concoction hit my bloodstream, steadying me, pushing out the chills I felt. It kicked my brain back into gear. My thoughts grew more coherent. I went over what I saw in the bathroom back at the rest stop and sucked in a deep breath.

"He's after me. The guy—the one who killed Susie—he said he's coming for me." Thoughts of where I could go and what I could do washed away rational thought. "I'm going to end up like Susie."

"We're not going to let anything of the sort happen." Griff pulled into a gas station that also had a fast food restaurant inside. "In there or here in the vehicle?"

"I don't want food. I have to figure out what to do so he can't get to me again." The words tumbled out, each one faster and more unintelligible than the one before it.

"He's not going to do it this second," Mysti said. "Let's get some food in you, and we'll talk about what you saw. Griff, go through the drive-thru."

He did and ordered what Mysti told him. I glanced around at all the other cars, expecting to see a man wearing a taxidermic, bastardized animal head get out of one of them. Griff took our paper sacks of food from the cashier and drove to a parking place. I didn't want the sausage biscuit they'd ordered for me, but they bullied me into taking a bite. Realizing how hungry I was, I ate two sausage biscuits and accepted a carton of milk. I sipped it, and normalcy crept back in.

"He knew my name." I shivered. "He shook the snow globe at me and said he'd see me soon."

"Who?" Griff closed the empty container his breakfast came in and set it aside.

I described the man I saw in the bathroom, my speech alternating between too fast and too slow.

Griff's face turned chalky. "Was it the same guy in the vision you had back at the motel?"

I recalled as much of the vision from the motel as I could, in as much detail as I could. Then I forced myself to think about the man who said he'd see me soon. The pearl snap shirt.

"He had on the same shirt in both visions."

"Think about the vision where you saw his face," Griff said. "Is there any chance he was someone we've met?"

Griff didn't dare lead me by saying Bobby John Culpepper's or Kevin Douglas's name, but I knew who he meant and shook my head. "It wasn't either of them."

"You're sure? Don't be afraid to tell me who it was." He half turned to stare at me. "I'll do everything in my power not to let him get to you."

"The guy wasn't Bobby John Culpepper or Kevin Douglas." I squirmed in my seat, trying to figure out how to explain what I'd seen and where I'd been. "It was like I was in the past and the present at the same time."

"What do you mean?"

"The guy I saw had Susie Franklin's corpse suspended over the toilet in the rest area."

Griff's eyes widened, and Mysti sucked in a breath.

"There's never been a body found in the rest area," Griff said. "I'd have seen reports of it in my research."

"She was dead," I said. "Real dead. Like her eyes had been cut out, and she'd been gutted. But here's the freaky thing. Her body was fresh. Blood was still dripping."

"So you went back in time?" Mysti stared at the back of the bucket seat in front of her, her words slow and thoughtful.

"Sort of. Maybe. I don't know." I blew out a hard breath. I couldn't quite form the words I needed to explain where I'd been. "The bathroom was new and clean, like it hadn't been used much."

"I heard you calling for us," Griff said. "What did you do to try to get out?"

"It was like once I got there, I was trapped." I used my hands to pantomime my words, irritated I couldn't verbally convey what I wanted to. "I couldn't get at the door to pull it open. There was this *thing* separating me from it."

"Like what?" Mysti furrowed her forehead.

"It...it was like pushing at something soft but impenetrable. These ripples of color would appear." I crushed my napkin in my fist. "It was like it was right on top of where y'all were." I paused, studying both Griff and Mysti's faces and seeing absolutely no understanding. "When Mysti started spelling, a rip appeared in the wall. The killer, it was like he knew what was about to happen. He shook the snow globe at me and said he'd see me soon." The snow globe. My link to Susie Franklin. Was it the killer's link to me, too? I remembered it going under the sink and then the killer tormenting me with it. *Where had it ended up?* I didn't see Griff or Mysti bring it out of the restroom. Half raising on my seat, I peered into the cargo area, searching for it. "Where is the snow globe?"

"We didn't see it in the restroom," Mysti said. "You must have left it in the other place."

"I've got a question about the visions," Griff said. "The first two, you were inside Susie Franklin, seeing the world from her point of view."

I thought about it a few seconds. "Yes. I was."

"But the last vision, you had a God's eye view. You watched the whole thing from above." Griff tapped his fingers on his legs.

"That's right."

"What if the killer sent you the last vision to lure you out to the rest stop?"

Cold worked its way through my body, raising goose bumps on my arms. I recalled the strong desire I felt outside the motel room to come to the rest area on my own.

"So the killer's a ghost?" Mysti glanced at me.

I tried on the possibility. It fit. Nobody but a ghost ever sent me a vision. I glanced between Mysti and Griff and shrugged. "Could be, but Susie had the snow globe when she got into the killer's car. The killer could have kept it when he killed her. If so, do we still think Susie's ghost put it in the bag Margaret Franklin gave us?"

We all stared at each other several minutes. None of us had any answers. Griff started the SUV and backed out of his parking spot. He didn't speak until we were speeding down the road to Nazareth. "Margaret Franklin recognized the snow globe as soon as she saw it. Let's find out everything she knew about it."

None of us said much on the drive to Margaret Franklin's house, but the air inside the SUV hung heavy with unanswered questions. Griff parked in front of her house, got out, and stalked toward the house. Mysti and I scurried behind him, almost running to keep up. Griff raised one clenched fist and banged on Margaret Franklin's door. When she didn't answer after a minute or so, he banged again, this time hammering until we heard footsteps. She opened the door, eyes droopy with sleep.

"W-wh-what is it, Mr. Reed? Is everything okay?"

"I'd like to ask a few questions about the snow globe." Griff almost danced foot to foot in agitation.

A car crept by on the street. I kept my back to it but felt whoever was inside staring.

"May we please come in?" I took a few steps to stand beside Griff. Margaret held open the door.

"Come in the kitchen," she said. "I still haven't had coffee."

We sat at a dainty breakfast set in front of a bay window. Margaret chattered at us while she made coffee, but none of us answered. Once she had the coffee pot gurgling, she joined us, her mouth set into a wary line.

"What's this about? I feel like I've done something wrong." She crossed her arms over her chest.

"I had another vision of Susie." I tried to pick my words carefully. "I saw her walking down a road, and the snow globe was visible in her duffle bag. She took it with her."

"Is that all you saw?"

Griff nodded yes for me.

"I need to know everything you can tell me about that snow globe, Margaret." I stared at her face, searching for guilt or fear. I saw nothing but confusion.

"Gosh, it was just a cheap old thing," Margaret said. "We saw it at a rummage sale hosted by the First Lutheran Church. Susie saw it and *had* to have it. Loved it ever since."

My shoulders rounded. It could have come from anywhere, from anybody. The coffeemaker beeped, signaling the coffee was ready to drink. Margaret stood and shuffled to get her first cup. The sound of liquid pouring into a cup drifted over from the kitchen. "Anybody else?"

"We're all coffeed out, I think." Griff managed a polite smile. "Do you know anything else about the snow globe?"

Margaret rejoined us, took her first sip of the day, and sighed. "The snow globe belonged to Lucille DeVoss. There was a whole set of 'em, each one a different city." She held the warm mug between her hands. "Lewis said he was selling them because he couldn't stand to look at them any more after she passed."

DeVoss. I rolled the name over in my mind. It sounded familiar.

"Oh, Susie loved that snow globe when she was little. Then, after her trouble with Coach Bobby John, it came out again. She'd spend hours and hours looking into it. Once I even..." Margaret trailed off and shook her head.

"Tell us?" Mysti gave her the sweetest of smiles.

"During that awful time, I used to hear her upstairs talking. She'd always stop when she heard me walking up the stairs." Margaret stared into the blackness of her coffee. "But one time, I snuck up on her. She was talking into that snow globe, like she was having a conversation with somebody."

Sweat broke out over my scalp, and my lips began to tingle. "Had she always talked to the snow globe?"

"That was the first time I ever heard her doing it." Margaret tapped at her cheek. "When she was little, it used to be her Barbie doll's aquarium. The imaginary fish that lived in it was named DeVoss, since the globe used to belong to Lucille DeVoss."

DeVoss again. Where had I heard the name? "Why does the name DeVoss sound so familiar?"

"You probably saw his signs as you drove into town. He owns all the land on both sides of the road for a good stretch. Sells both cattle and hay."

And drives his tractor down the road where people might hit him. Lewis DeVoss was the first Nazarite I met.

————

"W*e* *need* to talk to Lewis DeVoss." Griff started the SUV and pulled away from the curb. "By the way you two acted back there, you know how to find him."

"Wherever he lives, it's near the rest stop." A shiver worked its way through me.

Griff tapped the brakes and turned around in his seat. He stared at my face. "You're serious."

"More than," Mysti said. "Not real sure where his house is, but he owns all the land."

"And how do y'all know this?" Griff drove a few blocks until we sat in front of the Nazareth Area Public Library.

"He told us. I nearly hit him when we were driving into town. Remember I told you about seeing the people with burlap sacks over their heads and we decided it was that missing family? Well, I almost hit Lewis DeVoss right after I saw them."

"Shit," Griff muttered. "And you were going to tell me this when?"

"Mysti knew. I figured she'd tell you if it mattered."

"It matters." Griff took out his cigarillos and lit one. He offered me the pack, but I took out my own smokes and lit up. He glared at Mysti, then at me. "Is there anything else either of you'd like to tell me?"

"Oh, come on," I said. "You wouldn't have wanted to question Lewis DeVoss if I told you about him within the first five minutes we met."

"But I might have done more research on him. Give me my bag." He held out his hand.

"You mean your man purse?" I pulled the messenger bag from the cargo area and handed it to him.

Griff stuck his cigarillo in his mouth and clamped his teeth down on it. He grabbed the bag from me, took out his laptop, opened it, and plugged in his Internet anywhere card. He clicked keys for several minutes. Mysti and I sat in tense silence. His ass-chewing, while deserved, hadn't been any fun.

"Griff, I'm sorry. My excuse is I see so much weird shit

that I tend to let most of it roll off." I had a feeling there was no way he'd hire me after all this, but I couldn't give up. I needed to try to make it right.

"Fine," he said. "Don't do it any more when you're working for me. Tell me. I won't complain even if I can tell right away it won't help."

It wasn't forgiveness, but it was an indication he might hire me again. I relaxed a little.

"Lewis DeVoss lives at 5467 State Highway 231." Griff punched the address into his GPS and waited to see if it showed up. "Let's get over there before he leaves the house to work on his ranch. We'll never find him if he's plowing the back forty somewhere." He eased back into traffic and headed toward Lewis DeVoss's house.

"If nobody else is going to say anything, I will." Mysti half turned in her seat so I could see her face while she talked. "Lewis is alive. How could he be in Peri Jean's vision and be in the present day world as well?"

"Bilocation. The ability to appear in two places at once." Griff shrugged. "Look, I don't know much about it, but there's some mention of it in Greek philosophy. Aleister Crowley could reportedly do it."

Again, Griff's knowledge of weird stuff struck me. Exactly who was this man, and what was his connection to magic?

"If we want to call Peri Jean's visions a form of dreaming, which I'm not necessarily doing," Mysti said, shooting me a weak smile, "Matthew Hopkins described something similar in *The Discovery of Witches.*"

"So we're going to agree it's possible?" Griff glanced in the rearview mirror, meeting my eyes. "Consensus?"

"I'll agree, but I still can't fathom how it would work," I said. "The only beings with which I've ever interacted are spirits."

"Let's not let ourselves get bogged down in the how." He glanced at Mysti. "We've seen things on jobs I refuse to believe, and I saw them."

Mysti nodded in agreement. How many of Griff's cases were paranormal? Now wasn't the time to ask.

"My big issue is DeVoss's age." I unbuckled my seatbelt and scooted forward so I didn't have to raise my voice. "The man Mysti and I met didn't seem too athletic. You said the most recent disappearance was this year, right, Griff?"

"Three months ago. A college-aged woman." He rattled off the information, never taking his eyes off the road.

"I don't think Lewis DeVoss could have easily subdued someone young and fit." I called my memory of him, still seeing nothing more than a tired old man. "Unless he was faking the other day."

"Let's talk to him," Griff said. "He may be a dead end, but that snow globe is a weird little footnote. I can't leave it alone."

We were silent the rest of the drive. Lewis DeVoss lived at the end of a two-mile-long white sand road so rutted driving over it felt like being caught in a drum kit. We pulled up in front of the house in time to see Lewis DeVoss headed across the pasture to his barn. He didn't seem to hear our approach, so Griff honked. Lewis spun and almost lost his balance, then stomped toward us frowning. We climbed out of the SUV. DeVoss's facial expression softened somewhat as he recognized Mysti and me, but then Griff came around the SUV's side. DeVoss nearly stopped in his tracks. He approached us slowly.

"Ladies, good to see you again. Can I interest you in some honey? Canned figs? Don't do 'em as good as my Lucille, but they're passable." DeVoss glanced at Griff, offered him a small smile, and turned his attention right back on Mysti and me.

"Mr. DeVoss, I'm Griffin Reed of Reed Investigations." Griff marched over to DeVoss and held out his hand. The older man glanced at Mysti and me and reluctantly shook hands with Griff.

"Lewis DeVoss. Surely you folks didn't come to buy hay or a Black Angus cow?"

Griff turned to me and nodded. He expected me to talk? *Umm, okay.* I cleared my throat so DeVoss would turn his attention to me.

"When we met the other day, we mentioned we were working for Margaret Franklin in relation to Susie Franklin's disappearance back in 1980."

"Yep. I remember you's working for poor Meggy." DeVoss nodded and glanced back at his house. "As I ain't getting no work done, y'all want to come inside, enjoy the air conditioning?"

We agreed and followed him inside. He showed us to the living room, an oversized room with cathedral ceilings and exposed beams. Built-in bookcases lined the walls, filled mostly with framed pictures and decorative storage boxes. The brown wall-to-wall carpet was about ten years past needing replaced and smelled like it. Griff, Mysti, and I sat on a plaid couch so worn the cushions showed through in butt shaped spots. Lewis DeVoss sat on a matching recliner bleeding yellowed stuffing.

"So this is about Susie's disappearance?"

I glanced at Griff, who motioned me to go on and talk.

"Sort of. It's about a snow globe Susie Franklin owned. Margaret said she bought it at a church yard sale, and it originally belonged to you."

Lewis started nodding about halfway through my recitation. "Know just the one. Camden—my son—was furious I sold his mama's snow globes. They were older than him. His mama bought them when she was a teenager on a cross-country vacation." He worked his mouth and shook his head. "Pulled such a fit, I went back to get 'em. Embarrassed the hell out of me."

"They'd all been bought?" I asked.

"Nope. They's all still there, except for the one Meggy bought Susie. I's so ashamed I bought the damn things." He snorted and shook his head again. "You believe Camden wanted me to go ask Meggy Franklin for the last one back? I couldn't do that. Susie was just a little girl. Woulda broke her heart."

This was going nowhere, and I didn't know where to take it. "Does your son still have the other snow globes?"

DeVoss shook his head. "He ain't got nothing no more. He went off to college in New Mexico. Never saw him again."

So Camden disappeared? What did DeVoss mean? I raised my eyebrows at Griff in a silent plea for help.

"Did Camden still have the snow globes at the time he disappeared?" Griff asked Lewis DeVoss.

The old man shook his head and scratched his ear. "I never found 'em."

"How long's it been since you heard from Camden?" Griff fixed his gaze on DeVoss, staring at him so intently I was glad it wasn't me getting stared at.

DeVoss rocked back in his recliner, staring at the dusty beams on the ceiling. He laced his hands over his ample gut and became so still I watched his chest to make sure he kept breathing. Griff, Mysti, and I exchanged puzzled glances. The time crept by. I occupied myself looking at the pictures on the wall.

A few showed a much younger Lewis DeVoss with a bouffant wearing wife and a shaggy haired pre-teen son. *Where have I seen him?* He'd be all grown up, but we don't change much. I spotted another picture of the same kid wearing a cap and gown, but it was across the living room. I couldn't make out the kid's features. I kept returning my gaze to the picture of Camden DeVoss before he reached adolescence. There was something about him. Quietly as I could, I stood. Griff raised his eyebrows. I crept across the room to take a look. I choked on my own spit. Camden DeVoss's features had sharpened, and his eyes had hardened. I knew this man. I spun to face Griff. At the same time, DeVoss sat up straight.

"I'm going to tell you folks something nobody in this town knows." He leveled his gaze on Griff. "Hopefully, it'll clear up some matters for you. But I'd like your promise you won't gab it all over town."

I motioned at Griff, but he gave me a sharp head shake. "You have my word, Mr. DeVoss."

"My son's dead. Graduated high school in 1975. Got into a college in New Mexico. Couldn't wait to get away from me. Died in a car wreck the same year." DeVoss frowned at the couch and searched the room for me, finding me standing in front of his son's graduation picture. His mouth opened and closed. "That's my Camden. He never got no older."

I turned back to study the picture, seeing more of the guy I saw carrying Susie Franklin's body in my vision with every second.

"Got his death certificate right in this-here box." DeVoss appeared next to me and reached for a blue box sitting next to Camden's graduation picture. He approached the couch and set the box on the long, low coffee table in front of it. He took out a piece of parchment paper lying on the top and handed it to Griff, who glanced at it and handed it back.

"I'm so sorry for your loss, Mr. DeVoss." Griff's red-tipped ears and the strawberry splotches on his neck indicated a different emotion, but I didn't blame him for trying to save face. "I have one question, if you don't mind."

Without speaking, DeVoss drew a glossy photo from the box and set it on the coffee table for all of us to see. I walked over to get a clear look at it. The car was nearly smashed beyond recognition, but I recognized it as the one from my vision. My heart rate picked up to the level of discomfort. Sweat broke out on my back. I did everything I could to stay outwardly calm.

"I bet I can guess your question," DeVoss said. "Why'd I tell everybody he was missing, right?"

Griff nodded, the redness from his ears spreading onto his face to perch high on his cheeks.

"Before I lost Camden, losing my Lucille—my wife—was probably the worst thing I ever had to experience. But you know what made it worse?" He paused for a few seconds as though one of us might want to guess, but nobody did. "Townsfolk trying to help me feel better. Oh, they meant well, but they like to have drove me crazy. Got where I didn't want to talk about Lucille, didn't want to think about her, didn't even want to look at her stuff."

Which explained why he tried to sell her snow globes. I stared again at the wreck of Camden's car, half listening as Griff thanked DeVoss for his time. Mysti bought several jars of canned goods and a huge jug of honey. I moved along in a dream, waking when DeVoss grabbed my arm.

"I wanted to thank you for coming out to see me." He flashed the straight, perfect line of his dentures. "It sure was good to see your pretty face again."

"Thank you, Mr. DeVoss." I tried to smile and hoped it was good enough.

DeVoss opened the back door of the SUV for me, and I climbed inside, eager to get away from him. Griff and Mysti got inside, and Griff started the engine. He turned, a huge grin splitting his face, to speak to me.

"Don't say anything until we get away from here, okay?"

The look on his face set my nerves on high alert, but I nodded my agreement. The silence in the SUV made the drive back out to the main highway seem to take forever. Finally, we were on the road back to Nazareth.

"The guy in the picture." The upper part of Griff's face appeared in the rearview mirror. "He was the one in your vision, wasn't he, Peri Jean?"

"How'd you know?"

"Girl, you turned the color of oatmeal when you saw it." Griff sped toward Nazareth.

"Did you see her knees buckle?" Mysti spoke to Griff. Then she turned to face me. "Good job on getting control of yourself. I thought you were going to lose it right there and spill it all."

"Nah," Griff said. "I knew our girl had it under control." He pulled into the motel parking lot and unbuckled his seatbelt. "Being as you're our official medium on this job, let's hear your theory on what's happening."

"It's got to be Camden's ghost," I said. "Susie talking to the snow globe after her trouble with Coach Bobby John, my seeing him in a vision like that. It all adds up. But I've got one problem. I don't see how he's getting hold of people who aren't mediums like me."

"I think it's a good idea we talk to some people who knew Camden before he died," Griff said. "Let's see what he was into as a teenager. Hell, he might have had some sort of psychic gift himself."

6

———

Griff set up an office of sorts in his motel room with his laptop and his cellphone.

"I'm going to be making phone calls and accessing whatever databases I can on my computer." He pulled out a legal pad and tore off the top sheet of paper and handed it to Mysti. "Your job is to call Camden's college. Confirm he went there in fall of 1975. Something doesn't feel right to me about DeVoss's story."

"Am I looking for anything in particular?" Mysti took out her cellphone and her bluetooth earpiece.

"Unfortunately, it's needle in a haystack time. I'm looking for any odd stories about him, anything that doesn't quite fit."

"How will this tell us if he was psychic?" I stood by the door, useless as a condom on a stone statue.

Griff turned to me. "It won't, but it'll give me an idea of how dangerous this guy was." He paused to type something on his computer. He stopped and glanced at me.

"You call Margaret Franklin. She likes you best of the three of us. See if she can think of anybody who'd remember what Camden DeVoss was like. A teacher would be good. A classmate would be even better. Find out if Camden had an interest in the occult, or if there were odd stories floating around about him."

I left the room to call Margaret Franklin. She put me in touch with Donny Wayne McClure, who'd taught Camden senior level English.

"Now Donny Wayne is eighty-five if he's a day, but he's scary sharp." Margaret chuckled over the phone, her voice crackling. "Remembers things from back then better than he knows what he had for lunch. I'll call him on your behalf."

Margaret said her goodbyes and called me back a few minutes later. "He can't wait to meet you. Says he'll be waiting at the front door."

Donny Wayne McClure lived in an assisted living community a half hour's drive from Nazareth. The facility looked like a plain old nursing home to me. I parked and hurried to the front door.

A man who'd been sitting on the bench out front stood, leaning heavily on his cane. From a distance, he looked like a strong wind might blow him over. I got closer and realized only his body was frail. His blue eyes were clear and lively.

"You Peri Jean Mace?" He had a high, wheezy voice.

"Yes, sir. You must be Mr. McClure."

"Call me Donny Wayne. I've not been a teacher for going on twenty-five years." He bared a set of tobacco stained teeth at me and held out an age spotted hand. His skin was shiny and so thin it seemed I could see every vein. I was afraid to touch him, but the strength of his handshake surprised me. "Do you mind if we sit out here, hon? Fascists who run this place won't let an old man smoke inside his own apartment."

"Not a bit," I said and sat down on the bench. I took out my cigarettes and held out the pack to him. He shook his head and produced a pack of unfiltered Luckies. We both lit up.

"Margaret says you're looking into Camden DeVoss as part of an investigation on her daughter's disappearance. Mind if I ask why you think your firm can find Susie when nobody else could?"

His question made perfect sense, but it surprised me all the same.

"It's crazy, and you won't believe me."

"Try me." He blew a smoke ring. "I taught kids from the time I was twenty-three years old to the day I retired at the age of sixty-eight. I saw it all."

"I consult for Reed Investigations as a psychic medium." I waited for him to tell me his religion precluded any such nonsense and for the visit to go downhill from there.

"Do you now?" He stared at me so intently I squirmed like a high school kid who'd forgotten her homework. "And I take it you've contacted Susie Franklin's ghost."

"Her spirit made contact with me." Again, I waited for the bad stuff.

"Despite my confidence otherwise, Peri Jean, you have

managed to surprise me." He pinched his cigarette and tossed it.

"What do you think Camden has to do with this?" Donny Wayne regarded me out of the corner of one eye. "I have good reason to believe he's dead, was dead years before Susie disappeared."

"Lewis DeVoss showed us a death certificate for Camden." I checked Donny Wayne's expression for surprise, but he closed his eyes and nodded. *Did old Mr. DeVoss trot that thing out every time someone cornered him about the subject of Camden?* Something flopped around in my mind, but I couldn't catch it, and it disappeared back into the depths. "But I also saw…" I let my words trail off. I didn't know how to tell this nice old man I thought I saw a ghost kill a living person.

"I see from the look on your face you believe you're on the right path." Donny Wayne's stare slipped off me and contemplated the stained concrete walk at our feet.

"Mr.—Donny Wayne, I promise you we're not out to do Lewis DeVoss any harm or—"

McClure held up one hand and shook his head. "I'm an old man. Holding in what I know, what I saw, won't serve any purpose anyway." He cleared his throat and began talking in his whispery voice. "I taught Camden for both his junior and senior years of English. He was a straight B student, not because he lacked intelligence to be at the top of the class, but because his interests lay elsewhere."

"Sports?"

"He played football, and it got him a scholarship, but no." Donny Wayne crossed his arms across his wasted body. "Camden DeVoss thought he could bring his mother back from the dead. He believed he communicated with Lucille's spirit through the snow globes."

I jerked against the bench and dropped my cigarette lighter on the ground.

"You all right?" Donny Wayne raised one bushy eyebrow at me.

I leaned down to pick up my cigarette lighter and noticed my arms were covered with chill bumps. I rubbed the skin, though warmth wasn't the problem.

"I'm okay. Had a long few days." I quit rubbing my arms. The chill bumps weren't going anywhere. "Lewis DeVoss told us how upset Camden got when he tried to sell the globes in a church rummage sale. What you said made it all make sense."

"Ahh, yes. The fateful rummage sale of 1973. Lucille hadn't been dead for too long then, and Camden was really hurting. I take it you've met Lewis DeVoss?"

"I have," I said.

"Then you know he's a taciturn man, one who'd likely not be a great deal of comfort to a mourning teenage boy. His solution was to clean out Lucille's belongings, to forget her. If anything, Lewis's desire to forget his wife fueled Camden's need to reconnect with her." Donny Wayne shook his head and held up one hand. "Hate this worn out old brain. It gets side tracked so easily. Tell me something, Peri Jean. Have you *seen* one of the snow globes?"

"I saw the one Margaret Franklin bought for Susie at the rummage sale. Cheap plastic ones, looked like something sold to tourists. It had the name of a city in it." I considered telling him Susie used the snow globe to contact me, but I couldn't quite make myself say the words. Not after hearing Camden used them to contact the spirit world. My mind didn't want to accept the possibilities.

Donny Wayne stared at his lap and plucked at the material of his pants. Was he getting tired? Getting ready to have a stroke?

"How did that come to be in your possession, Peri Jean? I ask because I know Margaret couldn't find it after Susie went missing."

"It just sort of turned up." Dread sank into my stomach like a poisonous fishhook. What sleeping monster had I awakened by fooling with that snow globe?

Donny Wayne nodded. He reached into his pocket to get his cigarettes. His hand shook so badly I had to light one for him.

"Do you need something to eat or maybe some juice?"

"Nope. I ate right before you came. You've given me a bit of a fright."

My stomach curled in on itself and did a long, slow cartwheel. "How so?"

"I attempted to counsel Camden on the loss of the snow globe Margaret purchased for little Susie. My attempt greatly amused him." Donny Wayne pinched what was left of his cigarette between his thumb and forefinger without speaking. "He said one day little Susie would get a nasty surprise."

A huge man dressed in orchid colored scrubs stepped out on the porch with us. "Mister Donny Wayne, Nurse

Simmons is looking for you. She said she best not find you out here chain smoking."

"I'll be right inside, Terrence." Donny Wayne smiled at the younger man. "Come by later for a cappuccino."

Terrence gave us a wave and disappeared inside.

"Nurse Simmons is awful, Peri Jean, so I really must cut short this visit. However, I have two final things to share. The first is I advise you to look up Ollie Bickley back in Nazareth. He was the closest Camden had to a best friend in school. They had a very odd falling out in spring of 1975. The second is more of a question. Did Camden DeVoss manage to give Susie Franklin a nasty surprise?"

"The nastiest." I stood and held out my hand. Donny Wayne shook it. Terrence appeared like magic and helped the old man inside.

I drove back to Nazareth trying to make sense of the things Donny Wayne told me. Whether or not Camden was a natural medium like me, I knew he could have made the snow globes do anything he wanted with the right kind of magic. *Maybe the magic was already there.* I thought over the possibility but couldn't figure out who'd bother to spell the cheap snow globes. They certainly weren't a TV movie quality magical object.

I was more bothered by the idea Camden let Susie Franklin keep the snow globe planning to use it to hurt her. Had he already known in 1973 how he'd do it? I thought back to Kevin Douglas telling us he thought Susie'd met someone new and the way Susie seemed to expect the old car to come pick her up in the vision.

I couldn't make anything fit together. By the time I got

back to the motel, my stomach was rumbling loud enough to pass for thunder. I knocked on the door of Griff's motel room, half expecting to hear either Griff or Mysti shout to come back later. To my surprise, Mysti opened the door right away.

"Was the trip worth it?"

"Yes and no." I told Griff everything I learned from Donny Wayne but added I couldn't make heads or tails of it. "He did tell me to contact an Ollie—"

"Bickley," Griff and Mysti said together.

"We're going to surprise Mr. Bickley at his place of business later this evening." Griff stopped talking to yawn. His yawn made me yawn. Mysti caught the bug too.

"Sounds like the two of you had a productive day too." I checked the coffee pot Griff brought in with him and found it empty. A wave of fatigue blurred my vision. I leaned on the cheap dresser.

"I got lucky." Mysti sat on the bed and curled her legs under her. "The head of registration at Camden's college actually went to school there at the same time he did. She remembered him well."

"I'm willing to bet he wasn't a very nice guy."

I yawned again. "Sorry." I sat down next to Mysti on the bed. I heard her talking but not her words and dozed off without really meaning to. An air horn blaring jarred me awake. I sat up straight, my stiff muscles creaking.

Griff, still sitting in the stiff chair with his head thrown back in sleep, jerked away with a yelp. He fumbled his cellphone and dropped it on the floor, where the alarm continued to blare. He grabbed it and shut it off.

"I'm sorry I fell asleep." I stared at the cheap, motel issue bedside clock and gasped. I'd slept three full hours. Embarrassment crept through the leftover sluggishness from my nap.

"We all needed it." Griff stood and stretched. "I'm going to get cleaned up. We've got time for a quick supper before we visit Mr. Bickley."

Mysti and I went to our room where we rushed through showers, putting on clean clothes, and applying makeup, hers more elaborate than mine. Griff met us in the parking lot. Several minutes later, we sat at a table in Nazareth's other diner, a place called Pop's, waiting on three bacon chili cheeseburgers. Griff said, "Should have come here the first night."

"Can I tell her what I learned?" Mysti stirred her straw in her root beer float.

Griff sipped his chocolate malt and nodded.

"You were right earlier at the motel. Camden wasn't a nice guy. Bad temper. Wouldn't do his work. Went off on one of the professors." Mysti stopped to take out a notepad covered with scribbles. "Camden had a running feud with this senior named Freddie Felder. Typical Big Man on Campus, by the sound of it. It apparently got pretty nasty. Freddie slipped Camden some kind of tranquilizer, made him up like a woman, and left him on display in front of the library."

I cringed. Nice guy or not, the prank must have humiliated Camden down to his DNA. The waitress brought our burgers, and we dug in.

"Louise—that's the woman from the registrar's office—

said Camden started a fistfight with Freddie Felder and lost." Mysti leaned away from her plate to read from her notes. "Then, once Camden figured out he was flunking, he had an old friend from Nazareth help him pack up his dorm room. The guy introduced himself to every woman he came across. Ollie Bickley."

"Donny Wayne McClure told me the two had a falling out while still in high school." I polished off the last of my burger, a little sorry it went so fast.

"Maybe Camden bribed him." Griff ate several fries at once. "We'll find out later. We haven't even gotten to the juiciest part. Tell her, sweetie."

Mysti pinked and read off her notes again.

"After Camden's supposed death, which was a whole other thing, Freddie Felder was found murdered on campus. Louise said it was really gruesome." Mysti gestured at Griff, who pulled his laptop out of his bag. He opened it and took it out of sleep mode.

"I couldn't find a picture, but here's what I got from the first cop on scene. Freddie was suspended over a toilet with his eyes cut out and had been gutted."

I pushed away my malt. The huge pile of food on my stomach rolled around drunkenly. I begged it to stay where it was. "What's this about Camden's supposed death?" I asked.

"The State of New Mexico doesn't have any record of his death. I was able to find reports of the car crash, including the picture DeVoss showed us, but there's no record anybody died." Griff signaled the waitress for the check.

"Shouldn't we go back and confront Lewis DeVoss?" I asked. The old man seemed the best authority on what really became of Camden DeVoss.

"No. Because I got a feeling about this Ollie Bickley, and I never ignore gut feelings." Griff gave the waitress several bills and stood. "Plus, he gets off work right about now. Good time to surprise him."

———

THE SERVICE STATION'S windows were dark when we pulled into the lot. I'd noticed the place several times as I criss-crossed through Nazareth because it still had the old pumps out front, the kind that didn't take credit cards.

Griff, ignoring the darkened building, climbed out of the SUV, went to the window and cupped his hands around his eyes to see inside. Mysti and I climbed out of the SUV and hung back. The place smelled like grease and old car upholstery, the kind of smell clothes picked up and kept until they were washed in vinegar.

Griff tapped on the window and waved.

Faintly, I heard someone yell, "We're closed. Come back tomorrow."

"I don't need my car worked on. I need to speak with Ollie Bickley." Griff motioned to Mysti and me. We approached warily. This close, I noticed the front door bore greasy handprints. If it got on my jeans, I'd have to demote them to work clothes, and I didn't relish the idea of garage sale scavenging for a new nice pair.

The door opened and a short wiry guy stepped out. His

mostly gray, longish hair blew in the wind, and he swiped a hand across his sun-freckled forehead. He stared Griff down and said, "You outta luck, Mister. They done come and repossessed the truck. If my ex wants more money, she's gonna have to get her a job."

"This isn't about any of that, Mr. Bickley." Griff handed Ollie a business card. "Among other things, I investigate missing persons. Margaret Franklin hired my associates and me to investigate the disappearance of Susie Franklin."

Whatever bravado Ollie had drained out of him, rounding his shoulders and shortening him by a good two inches. He stole a sidelong glance at Mysti and me and asked, "What y'all want with me?"

Griff glanced at me and inclined his chin so slightly I might have missed it had I not been staring right at him. I walked over to stand beside him.

"We want to ask you a few questions about Camden DeVoss." I spoke in the same tone of voice I used at my part-time bartending job. The one I used to get men to tip me. "I spoke with Donny Wayne McClure earlier today, and he told me you and Camden were tight in high school."

"Not tight," Ollie mumbled. "I had one of them Ouija boards and Camden wanted to use it."

Bingo.

"Mind if we come inside and talk to you about it?" Mysti sidled up to our little group and treated Ollie to a big smile. "I see you have one of those old Coke machines. It work? I'd love to get a Coke."

Without giving us a real yes or no, Ollie stepped aside and held open the door. I followed Griff inside.

The smell of sour sweat joined the odor of grease and old upholstery. I stiffened my face to keep the distaste off it. If I messed up this interview because I couldn't stand a little B.O., Griff would have my ass. For some reason, his reamings bothered me more than any from other bosses I'd had. Mysti went straight to the Coke machine, fed it quarters, and got a Coke in a bottle. Very retro. Ollie gestured at some plastic chairs and pulled himself up on a heavy wooden desk that might have been new around the same time John F. Kennedy was in office. Mysti, Griff, and I sat.

"Why did Camden DeVoss want to use your Ouija board?" Griff put his arm over the back of Mysti's chair.

"You done found out about me. I have a hard time believing you don't know why." Ollie lit a generic brand cigarette and blew out a jet of smoke. "Let's cut the shit and get down to business, all right? Ain't got no home to go to no more, but I want to be done with this."

"All right," Griff said. "I want to know anything you can tell me about Camden DeVoss's interest in the occult, especially dealing with the snow globe collection he inherited from his mother."

"I always knew this would come back up." Ollie shook his head. "Wish so many times I'd have never met the little bastard." He went to the Coke machine and got himself a Dr Pepper and popped the top before he spoke again. "First thing to understand is Camden come by his interest in the occult, as you call it, honest. His mama was a backwoods witch. She did a big business in fertility potions, was my understanding."

Griff, Mysti, and I exchanged glances. I couldn't believe nobody in town told us. Or maybe I could. Small towns could close ranks to outsiders, and if Camden's mother died in the early '70s, there might not be many folks around who remembered her well.

"Camden claimed his mama used the snow globes sort of like the way you hear about people using crystal balls." Ollie rubbed one corner of his mouth, leaving a smear of grease. "Mind you, I never seen 'em do any such thing. Camden was trying to make 'em do what he wanted."

"Donny Wayne McClure told me Camden believed he could bring his mother back from the dead." I spoke without thinking, forgetting Griff was the boss. I glanced at him, and he gave me a nod.

"Naw, he didn't believe that." Ollie curled his lip and wrinkled his nose. "He wanted to contact the old lady's spirit, get her to transfer her power to him. Thought he should have come by it, inherited it, when she died."

Oh, big distinction there.

"I had my Ouija board and an interest in darker stuff," Ollie said. "Natural kid's curiosity is all it was, really, but Camden was more into it. He picked up a book on summoning demons somewhere and wanted to enlist the help of a demon in inheriting his mother's powers."

"What, exactly, could Camden's mother do?" I asked. "I'm sure he wasn't interested in dispensing fertility treatments to childless women."

"I like you." Ollie pointed one dirty finger at me and

winked. "According to Camden, she could control prosperity and health as well. She was the reason Camden's daddy earned so much money doing what many others fail at."

"So Camden DeVoss wanted to get rich and live forever?" Mysti cocked her head at Ollie, frowning. "I ask because I have the same sort of business as Camden's mother. I can tell you it's not as easy as having a little magical umph."

Ollie started to speak, then put his knuckles to his lips. "What is it you people think Camden had to do with Susie Franklin's disappearance?"

Griff, Mysti, and I had a conference of gazes. We couldn't weigh the pros and cons with Ollie sitting right there in front of us. Mysti nodded first. I followed. Griff sat back in his chair and crossed an ankle over his knee.

"Peri Jean Mace here is a psychic medium." He gestured at me. "She had a vision of sorts in which she saw Camden carry Susie Franklin's body into the rest area outside town."

Ollie's mouth dropped open. He started to speak but choked. He coughed so hard spittle flew from his mouth. Griff leaped out of his chair and hurried to him. He grabbed Ollie's Dr Pepper off the desk and handed it to him. Ollie took a sip, sputtered, and took another sip. He seemed to catch his breath.

"I'm sorry. Just caught me off guard." He took a deep breath and belched. "Camden had a dark side. Started letting it come out once we got to know each other. He used to catch little defenseless animals on his father's place and kill 'em. Slow. He used to joke he wanted to kill a person. He'd laugh, only his eyes didn't laugh. Never." Ollie shivered.

"Did he ever act on his fantasies?" Griff leaned forward, his gaze fixed on Ollie.

"Not on people, least not in front of me. Camden and I quit being friends over his odd tastes, though." Ollie glanced at me, then at Mysti. "Hate to tell this in front of ladies."

"Please tell us," Mysti said. "The information might help."

"Camden had his book on summoning demons, and he thought all he needed to do was sacrifice an animal. He chose this stray cat that hung around the school. The teachers fed it, considered it sort of a pet." Ollie swallowed hard. When he spoke again, his voice was barely more than a whisper. "He cut the poor thing's eyes out while it was still alive, and then gutted it. It was a relief when it died. I never felt so ugly in all my life. I told Camden not to come around me no more."

"What did he do?" I asked, disgust and grief for a poor animal I never laid eyes on rolling through me.

"Laughed. Said I was about useless, and he was done anyway." Ollie stared at the concrete floor, his face long, lips turned down. He folded his hands in his lap and closed his eyes.

"He left you alone then?" Griff lit one of his cigarillos, spurring both Ollie and me to light up.

"Pretty much." Ollie nodded, his gaze still downcast.

"Then why did you help him move out of his dorm

room at college in New Mexico?" Griff took a pull on his cigarillo and let the smoke drift out of his nostrils.

For the second time that evening, Ollie deflated. "I think I've said enough."

Griff closed his eyes and shook his head. "Mr. Bickley, you don't want to fuck me around. Understand?"

"I can't tell you no more." Bickley stood and wiped his hands on his pants.

"What are you doing to keep this place open?" Griff stood. "Your divorce pretty much cleaned you out. You're living in this place. Everybody in town thinks you'll close any day." Griff shoved his hands in his pants pockets and let his words sink in. "What are you moving through this place? My guess would be guns or drugs. Seeing as you've got a felony conviction for manufacturing—"

"All right, all right. I didn't tell you everything about the night with the cat." Ollie's eyes were shiny with tears.

"What else happened?" I asked.

Ollie dropped his head.

Griff pulled out his wallet. Ollie's eyes widened. Griff tugged out a hundred-dollar bill and waved it at Ollie. He said, "Trade you."

Ollie hesitated just long enough to make me wonder and then snatched the money like a frog going for a bug. "Need this. Ex-wife is bleeding me dry."

"So what happened after Camden butchered the cat?" I eyed Ollie in a none too friendly way. If he thought he could cheat us, he was wrong.

"He done it in the woods behind the school. A little boy caught us. And when I say little, I mean he was a baby almost. So little he started crying." Ollie let out another breath and got even smaller. "Camden chased after him. Kid fell down. Camden fell on him. Grabbed him by the hair and bashed his head into a tree several times." Ollie paused. "Never told anybody that. Kept it inside all these years."

"Did Camden kill the little boy?" Mysti's voice sounded like it had no air in it.

"I didn't stay to watch." Ollie took in the expressions on our faces and held out his hands in surrender. "Now that's the truth. I ran like my life depended on it."

From what Ollie'd said so far about Camden DeVoss, it well could have. My skin crawled, and I felt dirty—the kind of dirty you can't clean off—after listening to Ollie's story.

"I ran until I got home to my mama and daddy's. Next few weeks, people looked for that little kid. Todd something-or-other. Never found him. No body, no nothing." Ollie's chest rose and fell too fast. "I never spoke another word to Camden DeVoss until he called me up wanting help moving. And even the way he caught up with me was some weird shit. I was living in this," he said, shaking his head, "commune, I guess you'd call it, in Dallas. Payphone in the hall rang one day, and it was Camden." Ollie stopped talking, thought something over, and started again. "You got to understand something. Nobody knew how to get in touch with me there. I'd fell out with my folks and didn't have no friends. Was on drugs pretty bad." He said it in the tone of voice of a man making a shocking confession. "After Camden and I quit being friends, I started having these dreams, awful dreams, and Camden was always in them. He'd do awful things to me. Only way I could get them quiet was to be stoned, so I stayed that way for several years."

"So you helped Camden move." Griff picked up the story again. "Anything unusual happen?"

"Camden got into it with this Mr. All-American type. The guy wrestled Camden to the ground, kidney punched him a few times." Ollie's gaze tracked back and forth as though he was watching the events unfold. "Camden got up, dusted himself off, and we left. He told me in the car that guy would pay."

I remembered what Mysti and Griff told me in the diner happened to the guy Camden had a college feud with. My half-digested food rolled again. I put my hand across my belly.

"Where did Camden move to?" I asked.

"Up in the mountains with some hippie. Got the feeling he was into occult stuff as much as Camden. Next thing I heard, Lewis DeVoss was telling everybody Camden was missing."

"Lewis DeVoss told us Camden died in a car wreck in New Mexico," Griff said.

"Never heard about it." Ollie shook his head.

"Do you think there's a possibility he's still alive? Maybe living somewhere close?" I lit the last cigarette I had.

"Naw. I think he's dead," Ollie said.

"What brought you to that conclusion?" Griff asked.

"I stopped about a year ago at the old rest stop. You

know how sometimes you need to go pee-pee, and you can't wait another second?" Ollie's gaze tracked around the room, stopping on each of us to make sure we understood that kind of urge to relieve ourselves. "That's how I was that day. Couldn't wait. Not even the ten minutes it woulda took to get home."

The hair on my head prickled as though it was trying to stand up. I thought I knew the compulsion Ollie experienced.

"So I pulled off on the side of the road and hiked back there for a little privacy." Ollie mimed walking fast, going as far as to make a desperate face to match his story. "I did what I needed to do, and when I was leaving it was like something pulled my glance to the restrooms. It was like a magnet drawing me." He shivered and gooseflesh pimpled his arms. "Anyway, I looked over there, and Camden DeVoss was standing there in the doorway to the men's room, motioning me over." Ollie stopped his recitation.

"Did you walk over there?" I wanted him to say he didn't because I didn't want to hear what happened if he did.

"Hell no, ma'am. I knowed I was looking at the devil hisself." Ollie rubbed at the chill bumps on his arms. "Y'see, Camden DeVoss hadn't aged a day since I dropped him off to live in the New Mexico mountains with that hippie thirty years ago. It had to be his ghost."

Cold fingers walked up my spine, and I began to tremble.

Our footsteps crunched on the loose asphalt in the service station's parking lot. None of us spoke. I still had the shakes over Ollie's last revelation. I kept picturing the scene in my head. Ollie there at the rest stop staring at someone he hadn't seen for a lifetime and realizing that someone hadn't aged.

Griff pushed the button on his key fob. The alarm beeped off, but the locks didn't disengage. Griff, frowning, grabbed his door handle and pulled. He gave us a sheepish grin.

"Must have left it unlocked. Got too excited, I guess."

We all got into the vehicle and buckled up. "I'll drive a few blocks and park. He doesn't need to see us sitting in the parking lot discussing him." Griff started the engine. He pulled into the parking lot of Nazareth Memorial Park, dark and deserted for the night. Griff rolled down his window and lit one of his cigarillos.

"Those still stink even with the windows down," Mysti said.

"You know you love it." Griff patted her thigh, and she swatted at his hand. "Who thinks Camden DeVoss is dead?" Griff raised his own hand. Mysti and I raised ours too. "What do we think about what we learned from Ollie? Peri Jean?"

"I think Ollie's lucky he had sense enough not to go in that restroom. He'd be on the missing list if he had." I jerked with aftershocks of my shivers but thought I was getting over it. Oh, hell. No point in lying to myself. I couldn't sit still, and the only reason I didn't light a cigarette was I had none left.

"Agreed," Griff said. "But, for the life of me, I can't figure out the logistics on this thing."

"I've got a theory, not necessarily on logistics," Mysti said. "I think all the people who've disappeared over the years made that rest area their last stop."

"I'll play the non-believer," Griff said. "Why would someone stop there? It's obviously closed."

"People might not see a closed rest stop. It might look brand new and open." I pulled out my empty cigarette pack and gazed at it, imagining the cool rush of nicotine hitting me. I could ask for one of Griff's cigarillos, but then they'd know how much Ollie shook me up. My oversized pride would allow no such thing. "I wish the two of you could have seen what I saw in the restroom. It was completely different than what we saw at first."

"I am thrilled we didn't see what you saw." Mysti offered me a little smile.

"I am too. You might not have been there to get me out." With those words, the last of the shakes left me. Maybe I didn't need cigarettes after all. I should try quitting again. *Who the hell am I kidding?* I nudged Griff and pointed at his pack of cigarillos. He handed it to me, and I lit one up. It tasted as awful as I figured.

"I'll buy your theory, except for one thing," Griff said. "We agree he uses the snow globes as some sort of portal, right?"

Mysti and I nodded.

"How did he introduce it into the belongings of each and every person who disappeared over the years?" Griff glanced between us. "I mean, we're talking quite a few people."

"I don't know," I said.

Mysti shrugged and shook her head.

"And not to beat a dead horse, but are we saying a ghost committed these murders?" Griff tossed his cigarillo into the parking lot and shook his head.

"I've had ghosts do some pretty mean things to me, but I always figured it happened because of what I am," I said. "I think a ghost maybe could kill me. But someone who isn't a medium?"

"One doesn't have to be as powerful of a medium as you to see ghosts or feel the phenomena they can cause," Griff said. "I don't have even a glimmer of what you and Mysti have, and I've seen a few. Some pretty mean."

Exactly what kind of investigations did Griff specialize in?

"Could the ghosts have hurt you, though?" I posed the

thought as a question, but I had my own theory. I wanted to see what Griff said first.

"Maybe. Depending on the circumstances." He turned to glance at me and bit his lip. "I'm guessing we both have war stories, right? You tell yours."

"When I was married to my first husband, we lived in a huge, old house. Over the years, it had housed several businesses. One of them was a mortuary. That place was so very haunted." I closed myself to the memories of my marriage and focused on what mattered. "Me being there made it worse, like it gave the spirits an outlet or something."

"There's one problem with this theory," Mysti said. "Camden would need someone on the living plane to help him manifest in the way he finds most satisfying."

"The most obvious choices for Camden's henchmen would be Lewis and Ollie." I went over what I'd seen around both men. Ollie had an Ouija board as a teenager. He might have the same sort of power I did. Something hit me. "Here's my question. Why would Ollie help Camden? He was afraid of him. You don't fake that kind of fear."

"Okay, his father then." Griff spoke slowly, more to himself than to us. "Issue there is I can't picture him doing any kind of spellwork, even if it was to help his crop along or to fix a sick cow."

"Oh, honey, don't be naive," Mysti said. "The family that spells together…" She trailed off. "I don't know a word to rhyme, but I'd bet almost anything the whole family was into magic of some sort."

"It's not too late to go out and confront Lewis DeVoss." Griff started the SUV.

"But what will we say? We can't go in there hollering about him practicing witchcraft." I snorted. "He'll shoot us. Mount our heads on the wall."

"The death certificate," Mysti said. "Thing's probably illegal if there's no record of it with the State of New Mexico."

"Eh. I'll think of something." Griff backed out of his parking space and cruised through Nazareth. Mysti and Griff kept up a steady chatter, speculating about Lewis DeVoss, at times arguing. I stared out the window at the passing town. Something felt different about the town, as though someone pulled a thin film over it while we were stopped at the park. Things seemed cleaner and newer. More cars lined the streets, and all of them were old ones.

"Wonder if they're having an antique car show tonight?" I asked. Neither Griff nor Mysti heard me, and I didn't bother to repeat myself. I had a feeling I recognized from dreams, the knowledge things didn't make sense mixed with a lack of concern. It would all turn out okay in the end.

Griff picked up speed as we left town. The feeling of unreality heightened for me as I stared out over the moonlit pastures. It seemed darker. Things moved in the shadows, just outside the edge of my vision. A few times, I thought I almost caught something before it blended into the nightscape, but I was always too late.

"Y'all, I think this is a bad idea." I raised my voice, but Griff and Mysti seemed locked in their own little world, separate from mine. I repeated myself. Griff glanced into the rearview mirror and his eyes widened.

"You sick, Peri Jean? Want me to pull over?"

"I don't know," I said. "Something's not right. It's like there's things I can't quite see. Shadows."

The rest area came up on the right. It took me several seconds to realize what was wrong. The place was lit up like opening night at a catfish buffet, the kind where kids ate free. Griff let off the gas and put on his turn signal.

"Don't stop," I yelled. If Griff stopped, we'd disappear forever. Suddenly, I had a really good idea what the people who disappeared saw.

"What? Don't stop? Why? I don't want you puking in my ride." He pressed down on the brakes. Next to him, Mysti drew in a whooping breath.

"Don't stop." Panic raised her voice. "Don't stop. It's a trap." She swatted Griff's arm.

"What the…" Griff gunned the engine, shooting past the rest stop. The sudden takeoff made something roll out from underneath his seat. The snow globe came to rest against my feet. All the oxygen left my body, and all my spit dried up. My heart stuttered and roared to life. I wanted to tell Griff or Mysti, but I couldn't move.

At my feet, the snow globe lit up. Inside was the rest stop at night. A car sped through, leaving a green blur, and disappeared. He was coming. Camden was coming. I had to warn Griff and Mysti.

I commanded my hand to reach down and pick up the snow globe so I could show it to the others. It lay in my lap, immobile and numb. Mentally, I shook myself. I couldn't freeze up like this. Not when other people depended on me.

"Griff," I croaked.

"What is it?"

"The snow globe's back here with me. It's showing the rest stop. I saw—I mean, I think I saw—Camden's car leave." I sucked in a shaking breath. "He's coming after us."

Griff glanced in the rearview. "I don't see him. Maybe if we make it out to the main highway..." Griff pressed down on the accelerator, and the big engine responded with a roar. We shot through the dark night, headlights showing a little of the road ahead at a time. The headlights caught something shiny, just a flicker. Then, out of the darkness, Camden's ugly old car appeared. Griff slammed on the brakes. The tires squalled their displeasure. The car still rushed toward us.

Too late. Too late. Too late. My mind cried the words over and over like a song caught in my head. Mysti's scream rattled my eardrums, and I tried to brace myself. Fear gripped me so hard my jaw hurt.

"Noooooooo," Griff yelled.

We hit Camden's car. Loose items flew forward. My seatbelt bit into my chest and forced the air from my lungs. I had a second to watch the SUV's hood crumple and a spider's web of cracks appear on the windshield. Then my head snapped back at the impact, a sunburst of pain forming in my neck. I slammed back into the seat hard enough to wake up the old injury in my lower back. The world stilled, and I drifted.

———

THE SOUND of metal grinding together and shrieking jerked me awake. The world was black, the moon hidden by banks of dark clouds. The SUV began to move. I tried to call out to Griff and Mysti, but my chest hurt too bad. I drifted off again.

The squeal of a big door rolling up on a track woke me the second time. I sucked in a deep breath, and my ribs screamed in protest. The salty, metallic taste of my own blood running down the back of my throat and filling my mouth nearly gagged me. A little examination made me think I'd just bitten my lip or tongue. I opened my eyes. Bright, artificial light filtered into the SUV's windows. A thunderbolt of pain throbbed in the middle of my forehead, like my sinuses were full to bursting. Darkness flashed behind my eyes. My vision wavered. *Stop this, Peri Jean. Toughen up.* I couldn't afford the luxury of pampering my hurts. I rubbed my face hard and tried to shake it off. Now I could see the shape of Griff's shoulder and Mysti's head.

"You two alive?" I barely heard my own voice.

"Think so," Mysti said. "How did Camden do it? How'd he get the car around that curve and ahead of us?"

I didn't know, so I said, "Who pulled us off the road?" Ghosts can't tow vehicles. Someone on the living plane had moved the SUV.

Mysti moaned in answer to my question. The metal door I'd heard coming up slid down and hit the ground with a final sounding bang. Mysti and I both jumped.

"Griff?" I reached out and touched his shoulder but got no response.

"Is he…" I couldn't say it.

"No. He's breathing," Mysti said. "I think the airbag knocked him out."

"We gotta get out of here," I said. "Will your door open?"

"I can't leave Griff."

I dropped back against the seat. She was right. We couldn't leave him.

"Where's the shotgun?" I asked.

"I saw it go flying when we hit," Griff said, his voice thick. "You two okay?"

"My collarbone's hurt," Mysti said.

"I think I'm just bruised," I said. "What about you?"

"My knee hit the dashboard," Griff said. "I'm not going to be able to go far on foot. I want the two of you to go out the cargo door in the back and get help."

I knew Mysti wouldn't leave Griff without having to ask. No way in hell I'd leave them. Nazareth was a good five miles away. If I couldn't get a car to stop for me, I'd have to walk the whole way. The odds of me making it back in time to help Griff and Mysti were dismal. But I could find that shotgun and use it to protect us. I unbuckled my seatbelt and raised myself off the seat. Something punched into Griff's door and wrenched it open.

"Hold it right there, ma'am, and I mean don't move a muscle."

"He's got a gun, Peri Jean." Griff's voice cracked. "Sit back down."

I turned around and saw Lewis DeVoss pointing a huge, silver revolver at us. Large caliber too, judging by the chambers in the cylinder.

"I want you all three to step out of the vehicle." Lewis backed away from the SUV, far enough away he'd have time to shoot us if we rushed him.

"We're hurt. I'm not even sure I can walk," Griff said. I figured he was stalling, so I peered out the SUV's window, searching for weapons or exits.

Another car sat next to us. I squinted at it, knew I was seeing something familiar, but didn't know quite know what. My addled mind clicked into gear. It hit me. I bit back a silly, frivolous, unnecessary scream. Sometimes there is no help for horror.

Next to us sat the car we hit out on 231, the one Susie Franklin took her last ride in. The car was rusted out, on blocks, and had its hood up. It hadn't been anywhere in years. Though I already guessed the car was part of Camden's ghost realm, seeing it like this, obviously out of commission, spooked me more than Lewis DeVoss's hand cannon. Mysti saw the expression on my face and turned to see what I saw. She let out a long wail which expressed my feelings perfectly.

"Shut up." DeVoss issued the command in a conversational tone, sort of the same way you'd ask someone how they liked this weather.

Mysti continued howling. I didn't blame her. I wished I could do something to ease the tide of horror building in my mind and eating up all rational thought, but I couldn't even move. I was too scared.

"Shut her up." DeVoss stuck the gun in Griff's face. "And get both these women out of the damn vehicle."

I might have been about to die, but DeVoss's tone pissed me off. I yanked on my door, ready to confront him. The pain hit like a clap of thunder. The wreck had pulled something in my neck. I writhed in the seat, barely able to keep from whining. DeVoss opened my door and pulled me out. I dropped to the dirt floor of his barn hard enough to jar the air out of my lungs again. A beehive of pain took up residence in my side where the seatbelt bit into me. I gasped at the intensity of it.

"Come on, sir. Get on out," DeVoss said. "You make me shoot you, won't be no killing shot. I'll shoot that knee you're favoring. Shoot your lady in her hand."

I lolled in the dirt, trying to gather my strength. I thought I could fight Lewis DeVoss with Griff's help. Anger and defiance made me feel strong enough to lasso the world and whip it into submission. Mysti would help. The three of us could bring him down.

DeVoss walked off while I battled the haze of pain and fury clouding my head. Water splashed in a basin, but I couldn't turn my head enough to see. His footsteps came back. Cold water washed over me.

"Wake up, you stupid bitch. I ain't carrying you."

I heard a pop. DeVoss grunted and tripped over me. I wiped water out of my eyes in time to see Griff slide out of the SUV. He must have hit DeVoss with the door. Griff put his good foot on the dirt and held his other one aloft. I rolled toward DeVoss, searching the dirt for his revolver. If I could get my hands on it, we could beat him. DeVoss rolled over, and I heard the click-click-click of him pulling back the hammer on his monstrous revolver.

"All right. I'm done fooling around with you meddlers. Get your asses over there in those chairs by the time I count ten." He leveled the gun at my arm. "You don't, and I'm gonna be blowing off arms and legs. You'll live a long time 'fore you die, and it'll hurt even more'n it's going to."

I turned my head, worried by the cracking sound my neck made, to see where Lewis pointed. What I saw made me dizzy with fear.

Three straight back wooden chairs were backed up against a far wall. All three had shackles attached to the legs and the armrests. Near the shackles, the chair's wood bore deep gouges and scars. Dark spatters dotted the boards behind the chairs. Long lines trailed from the stains where something had run. *Blood. I bet it's blood.* My skin tightened.

I met Griff's gaze, and he nodded at me and mouthed, *Go on.* He turned away from me and went around the SUV to help Mysti out. She yelped in pain. A few seconds later the two rounded the vehicle, supporting each other. I found out how many of the muscles in my neck I used to get to a standing position. It screamed the whole damn time. The three of us limped to the chairs. We were going to die in this musty corner of Hell.

"Try not to look at the chairs," DeVoss said. "It'll make the waiting worse. Scareder you are, worse it'll be on the other side."

The other side. Did he mean Camden's killing room? "What's the other side?"

"Where you going." DeVoss followed us and began attaching the chairs to chains suspended from the metal ceiling beams. "Where you stepped into when you stopped in that stupid rest stop. You's a goner soon as he saw you through the snow globe, soon as he felt what you are."

"What does Camden think I am?" I asked.

"Power for him to eat and absorb. My boy's a smart one, he is." DeVoss stepped to the edge of the half circle and pointed his gun at us. "Now y'all sit in those chairs and buckle up."

We stared at him. I considered running again but knew I wouldn't be faster than a bullet. Plus, I couldn't leave Mysti and Griff. By the time I got back, it would be too late.

"Y'all gonna cooperate? Or am I gonna shoot out some kneecaps? Don't matter what I do to you, long as you're alive when I bring Camden in."

"Why are you doing this? Why are you letting your son do this?" Hysteria made my words tangle together, but DeVoss understood fine.

"This is my *son*," he said. "The last blood I got."

Terror, colder and more unforgiving than the darkest night of winter, swept through me, filling me, and choking off my sanity.

"My boy is lonely." DeVoss spoke slowly, as though to someone mentally deficient. "He gets urges. If the price of keeping my boy comfortable and happy is the lives of you three nosy-rosies, I'm okay with it." He pointed the gun at Griff, the biggest and strongest of us. "So what'll it be? Walk to the chairs on your own or force me to hurt you?"

Mysti, Griff, and I contemplated each other. Sadness elongated both my friends' faces. Mysti gripped my hand and gave me a tug. Griff limped toward one of the chairs. Mysti followed, and I brought up the rear. This was it, the way the world ended for us.

"All right. Pull the chains around your middles, and use the padlocks to secure yourselves."

"Mysti, darlin'." Griff's voice trembled. "I am sorry I gave you the run around about being in a relationship. I love you, and I wish I had done things another way." He brought the chain around his middle and clicked the lock.

"I love you too, Griff," Mysti said.

DeVoss waved his gun at Mysti and me. We buckled ourselves in for the ride. I didn't have anybody to say goodbye to, so I closed my eyes and tried to figure out what I was going to do once Camden pulled me back into the rest stop.

"I'll go get Camden," DeVoss said.

Go get him? My eyes popped open, and I stared at DeVoss, confused. I assumed Camden's ghost would summon us.

DeVoss pressed his lips together and sighed. "Look. This is really the only way this whole thing can play out. Once y'all fooled around the rest stop and Camden made contact with you, it was over. He'd have got you one way or the other. You see the wreck he caused you to have. This'll all be over with by midnight tonight." He turned and exited the building through a side door.

Midnight's four hours away. My nerves jittered and danced at the thought of what would happen over the hours to come. Too soon, I heard wheels squeaking their way toward the building. Sweat popped out all over my body. Images flashed behind my eyes, the worst things my imagination could conjure.

The big overhead door rolled up, and DeVoss rolled in a man in a wheelchair. He marched him through the room and rolled him to a stop in front of us and locked the chair.

"Here they are, son." DeVoss leaned forward and kissed his son's greasy, thinning hair. He stepped back a few feet.

The man in front of us didn't look like he could stomp a roach, much less hurt three healthy adults. Drool ran from one corner of his mouth, and his hands were fixed in claws. One eye rolled in its socket while the other stayed fixed on a spot somewhere on the bloody wall behind us.

"What do you do with all the bodies?" Mysti's eyes glowed too bright, and she held her gaze on Camden DeVoss as she asked her question.

"Buried 'em." Lewis DeVoss crossed his arms over his chest. "I own more than a thousand acres of land. Be near impossible to find 'em."

Anticipation gnawed at me. Part of me wanted to yell at both DeVosses to get it over with, but the other part still wanted a chance to fight, to survive. Lewis DeVoss walked in front of our chairs, setting a snow globe in front of each of us.

"All right, son. You can go ahead and pull the little black headed one in like you did before." Lewis DeVoss took a syringe out of his pocket. "I'll knock the other two out for you."

The edges of Camden's psyche tickled at mine. I strained against letting him in, pushed until my nose hurt and my breath came in pants. Sweat popped out under my arms. My ribs protested. I glared at the mangled man through narrowed eyes. He began to shake with the effort of forcing his way into my brain. Lewis DeVoss approached me, head cocked to one side. He struck like a snake, his big, gnarled old fist shooting out and burying itself in my stomach. The breath whooshed out of me. My focus waned for one second, and it was enough for Camden. He shoved into my innermost self, burning and ripping himself a path. My vision darkened, and my conscious tumbled down a dark tunnel.

I woke up on the floor of the restroom, mouth dry, entire body throbbing. The place sparkled, everything new and in working order. The sharp tang of bleach stung my nostrils, making my eyes water. I glanced at the window. As I watched, the night went gray with dawn, full daylight came and went, and the sky turned pink with the oncoming sunset all in the space of a couple of minutes. The ripple of iridescence covered the floor and shone over the walls, a bubble holding me in this timeless, isolated place.

I pressed the palms of my hands against the cool floor and raised myself to a sitting position. Water dripped somewhere, and I smelled the soap in the dispensers at the sinks. All four doors to the toilets were closed. Was I alone? I twisted on the floor so I could survey the whole room, sore tendons and muscles crying out from the abuse.

"They're not here yet." The voice came from within the

room, its deep bass notes bouncing off the tile walls. "Griff and Mysti aren't as easy to pull in as you are."

Judging by what I saw in Lewis DeVoss's barn, Camden was very much alive, so I couldn't fathom why we had a connection. I got slowly to my feet, body screaming in pain with every move. A movement in one of the corners caught my peripheral vision. I turned and gasped, suddenly getting a real good idea about the source of Camden's connection to me.

"Your victim's spirits are still here." The burlap head family watched me from one corner. A young woman with dark hair and rope marks around her neck stood near them, reaching out to me. The spirits thought I could help them. Their pull plus Camden's was more than I knew how to fight.

"When I'm bored, I come here and play with them," Camden said. "It's all mine, so I can move time backward, forward. Do it again and again."

My mouth went dry. If I died in this place, I'd stay as Camden's plaything.

"Okay, here we go." Camden's voice filled the room again.

Two wet slaps cut short my fear fest. Griff and Mysti lay on the floor, curled against each other. I scooted over and poked Mysti with one finger. She moaned and stirred.

"Wake up." They had to wake up and help me. I didn't know how to fight Camden on my own. Mysti would have some ideas. Griff would help us.

"We're all here. Let's get started." The metal stall door swung open, and Camden stepped out wearing the same bunny-horse head I'd seen in my vision. He yanked his special curved knife free of the battle-scarred sheaf on his belt and walked toward me. His tight jeans and engineer boots were a far cry from the clothes of his convalescing body in the real world. He took slow measured steps across the restroom, stopped a short distance from me and nudged me with his boot.

"C'mon." His deep voice still boomed both because of the small space and because of the way his mask muffled it. It sounded creepy and crawly, which was probably how he liked it. "Get moving. All of you."

The hair on the back of my neck rose, and my bowels turned to liquid. His voice held no more emotion than a man asking for a glass of milk. He didn't even sound angry.

"Mysti." I knelt and shook my friend's shoulder. No response. I tried the same thing on Griff, and he didn't move.

"Idiot, do you hear me?" Camden's loud voice bounced off the tile walls, echoing in on itself and coming back for more.

I jumped and gaped at him, not knowing what to do. =

Camden rushed toward me, yelling, "Didn't you hear me? I said 'run.'" He got close enough for me to smell the mildew on the horsey head he wore.

I recoiled and scooted backward toward the sinks.

Mysti stirred on the floor, reacting more to Camden's voice than she had to mine. She opened her eyes and struggled to a sitting position. She peered around the room, blinking stupidly. She saw Camden, and realization hit her. She put her hand to her stomach and moaned, "Oh no."

Ignoring Camden, I hurried to her side and pulled her to a standing position. I already had a theory on getting out of this, but I didn't know how to communicate it to Mysti. Camden wanted to see our fear. If we didn't show it to him, he might not be able to work up the juice to kill us. This dreamscape of his had to take serious mental energy. Eventually, he'd run out, and we could escape.

Camden strolled over to Griff, practically bobbing his head in joy, and reared back one of his engineer boots.

"Don't kick him," Mysti yelled.

It was all Camden needed. He let it fly. Griff's eyes flew open a second before the boot made impact. He grabbed Camden's leg and twisted. Crying out, Camden danced around, hopping on one foot. Griff gave his leg another twist, and he went down. Camden's breath rushed out of him in a pained yelp, and the iridescence coating the walls disappeared, showing us the filth of the ruined restroom underneath. Griff rolled to his feet.

"Run for the door," he screamed at Mysti and me. We raced for the restroom door. Griff reached it first, yanked it open, and herded Mysti and me through.

Feet slamming on the ground, breath tearing out of us, we ran for the parking lot. The day had gone to night again, and moonlight shone on the asphalt, reflecting back in puddles of yellow light. One car sat in the parking lot. It was Camden's old beater.

"Hurry." Griff pushed Mysti and me toward the car.

"But it's not here." I stopped running and pressed one

hand against my side where my smoke-singed lungs begged for mercy.

Griff whirled to glare at me. "What are you talking about?"

"It's back in DeVoss's shop on blocks. It's an illusion." Speaking instead of gulping precious oxygen made me dizzy. I ended up letting Griff tug me the rest of the way to the car.

"It's here. See? You're touching it." Griff jerked open the driver's side door and shoved the seat forward. "Get in before he comes after us. Now!"

Can't hurt to try. Plus, he's not going to listen to reason. I leapt inside. Griff got in. Mysti climbed in the passenger side.

"Key's in the ignition," he muttered.

"Because it's not real. It's all part of this mental torture chamber Camden created in his mind. It's—"

"There's got to be a way out of this hellhole." Griff started the engine and burned rubber backing out of the parking place. The car's engine roared in protest as we sped toward the rest stop's exit.

I didn't believe it was this easy to get away from Camden, but I couldn't stop myself from hoping. Maybe the exit would lead us back to the real world. I'd rather deal in reality than fight in some psychopath's playground any day.

The exit grew closer, and euphoria surged through me. We were going to make it. I could see the highway on the other side of the long driveway. As I watched, a modern-day sports car drove past. Just a little bit more. The nose of

Camden's junker left the rest area and disappeared into a ripple of intensely colored light. *No, no, no, no.* A sob of disappointment built in my chest.

"Hold on," Griff yelled. "Maybe we can push through." The engine howled as he pushed down the accelerator. The sparkling pool resisted.

For the first time, I became aware of the black opal swinging back and forth on my chest. I called on its power, feeling the zing of it spread through me, tingling as it made its way. The colorful pool resisted for a second and then accepted us.

The three of us sat on the restroom floor again. My disappointment burnt to a crisp and rebirthed itself as anger.

"Mother*fucker.*" I slapped my hand on the floor. The black opal still burned on my chest, but I had no idea what to do with its magic. I'd tried the only thing I knew, and my efforts put us right back where we started.

Camden launched himself at us, and Griff caught him mid-stride. The two men struggled, grunting with effort. I took a step toward them. I had to help. If I could distract Camden, maybe Griff could wrestle the knife from him, stab him. He probably wouldn't die, not in his playground, but it would hurt him, maybe weaken him. The weaker he got, the less time he could hold this place together in his mind. Then we'd be free to fight it out with his father. I danced around Camden and Griff, searching for my opening.

"It's okay." Mysti grabbed my arm, her voice stronger than I felt. "I think I know what to do. I need your help."

She led me a short distance away and began to speak so fast her words sounded like an exotic language in which I was almost, but not quite, fluent. "I'm going to start casting a circle. When I do, you yell for Griff to get in it with us. Then we're going to bind Camden from harming us."

Mysti started her routine, which was familiar to me after these weeks as her apprentice. When she was halfway through casting the circle, she nodded to me.

"Griff!" I shouted. "Get in the circle with us."

Griff changed gears more quickly than I'd thought him able. He shoved Camden, sending him sprawling. He leapt into the circle just a few inches to spare. Mysti closed it.

"It doesn't matter," Camden said. He crossed his arms over his chest.

"We'll see about that." Mysti pulled a thread off her blouse and took a business card from her pocket. With her finger she began tracing a word. Pulling on the power of the black opal, I stood near Mysti and placed my palm flat on her back. She gave no notice I'd touched her until the power hit her. Her finger left a charred trail on the business card. She went back over the first part of the word and "Camden DeVoss" took shape. Then she rolled it into a tube and tied the thread from her blouse around it. She took a deep breath and raised her arms. "Camden DeVoss," she yelled. "I bind you with your own evil."

Mysti's and my power filled the circle, with a light I felt rather than saw. Camden jumped at the circle, laughing when I flinched. We'd show him this was no joke. I glanced at Mysti, ready for her to put the butt-hurt on him.

"I bind you from harming the three of us." Mysti's soft

voice boomed with power. "I bind you from harming the souls you've trapped here. I banish you from this place and bind you to the real world, that you may be trapped there forevermore."

Camden's lips twisted, and his eyes bugged out. He clutched a spot on his chest. His sides heaved with hard breaths.

Mysti glanced at Griff and me. "Say it with me. Both of you."

We obeyed, the feeling of energy in our circle increasing.

Camden fell to his knees. A thin line of slobber ran out of his mouth and stretched to the floor.

"Come on." Mysti elbowed me. "One more time."

Griff and I spoke the words. Hot, bright power filled me until I thought I'd burst and become nothing more than a ball of light. Camden collapsed onto his side and jerked a couple of times. I sagged with relief and put my hands on my knees.

"All right. All we need to do is finish it." Mysti secured the rolled business card by tying three knots. "One of you give me your cigarette lighter."

Griff handed her the fancy blowtorch lighter he used on his cigarillos. Mysti set the card on fire, and it flamed bright, burning orange and blue. She dropped it on the floor and let it burn at our feet. I couldn't keep from glancing at Camden's still form. Something wasn't right. Shouldn't he disappear? Go back to the real world?

"I don't understand..." Mysti put her fingertips to her lips.

Camden flopped onto his back and barked laughter at the restroom's ceiling. He gained his feet and stood in front of us, clutching his sides, the ugly mask on his head bouncing with his chuckles. His guffaws went on and on, long enough to give me time to feel the first cold stirrings of terror. Maybe there was no way to beat this monster. Finally, his laughter died.

"Y'all were great." He pointed his knife at us. "It was all 'I bind you with this business card and thread' and 'Do no more evil.' Y'all believed that shit." He broke up again, choking on his own laugher. He didn't laugh as long this time. "Now let me show you what I can do." He stomped over to our circle. Using his knife, he cut through the air, making it bleed the iridescent ripples I'd come to associate with this place. He reached in and yanked me out.

The way he did it, like he was the Guru of Doo-doo and I was one of his little dingleberries, pissed me right square off. I faced him and threw back my shoulders, anger surging through me. "Go on. Stab me. Gut me. Cut out my eyes. Get it over with it. I'm sick of your bullshit."

Camden shook his head and took a step away from me.

"That's right. You won't do it because you didn't get to scare us enough." I jabbed a finger at Camden to punctuate my point, and he reached out and grabbed it, yanking me against him. I put my free hand on his chest and tried to shove away. It was like pushing on a ten-ton statue. One of his slimy arms snaked behind my back and held me fast.

"You will provide me entertainment, whether you like it or not." His extremely deep voice echoing inside his stupid bunny-horse head tickled my funny bone. It wasn't the right time to laugh, but I couldn't help myself. I brayed right at the horse's snout.

Camden let go of my finger and grabbed his knife from the sheath. He used it to cut a thin red trail down my forearm. Electric pain traveled with the knife. I squealed and tried to wiggle away, laughter the furthest thing from my mind. Camden jerked me against him again but immediately yelped and danced away.

"You burned me," he yelled. "How'd you burn me?"

"You cut me, you idiot," I shouted back. Truth was, I didn't know how I'd burned him. He rubbed a spot on his chest. The black opal shot a shock of magic through me as though saying, "Yeah. I did that." How had the black opal burned Camden when it was still cool on my chest?

It didn't matter right then. I saw a perfect opportunity. A lifetime of fistfights made me notice Camden stood legs wide apart, completely unprotected. I reared back my foot and kicked him hard enough to break those babies and make an omelet. It was like hitting a steel plate.

I fell to the ground, cradling my wounded foot and moaning, "Cock knocker," over and over again. Mysti scooted over to me and hovered over me as I tried to recover. Camden ran toward me, and Griff rushed at him. Camden slashed with his knife. Griff jumped away, eyes widening and filling with pain. A stripe of red seeped through his white dress shirt. He backed away from Camden, raising one hand to his chest.

My mind whirled back and forth. We couldn't run from

Camden. We couldn't magic him. We couldn't fight him. He was going to wear us down and torture us to death.

A sharp shock pinged at my chest. *The black opal's magic. It's letting me know it can help. But how?*

The woman who gave me the stone told me it enhanced my natural abilities. It sure hadn't helped increase Mysti's witchcraft-doing abilities enough to thwart Camden, and I didn't see how enhanced ghost-seeing would help us.

The stone sent another shock into my skin. Then another. *If I concentrate on the magic and let it do what it wants, how much worse off could I be? If I do nothing, I'll die here. Mysti and Griff, too.*

I glanced up at my friend who still hovered over me, ready to die fighting Camden to protect me.

"The black opal," I whispered. "I think it has an idea."

"What?"

"I don't know." The pops of magic stung my skin at regular intervals. "But you might want to get away from me."

Mysti scooted backward, grabbing Griff's arm as she went. She motioned at the sinks, and the two of them slid underneath the porcelain bowls. I clutched the black opal in one hand and shut my eyes tight, feeling for the sharp sting of magic, ready to latch onto it. *There it is.* I felt the magic traveling through the stone and jumped when it sank through the palm of my hand. A low rumble came from the back of the room where the toilet stalls were. Water bubbled in the basins.

Oh, no. All I've managed to do is back up the sewer system. I braced myself for a shit shower and held my breath.

An earth-shattering crack shook the room. From my vantage point, I could see each toilet had split in half. The porcelain bowls falling had made the awful noise.

"What the fuck?" Camden watched the whole thing from inside his horsey-head. All I could see were wide, surprised eyes.

A long crack appeared in the concrete, accompanied by a rending sound I didn't like one bit. Never letting go of the black opal, I slid underneath the row of lavatories with Mysti and Griff. Their wide stares and pale faces suggested I'd fucked up royally. The crack in the concrete widened, letting in a spill of deep green light. At first, the iridescent waves of Camden's dream world pushed at the green, driving it backward. Then the crack widened again, and the green seeped into the room. The green was almost opaque, but I saw shadows moving within it. One of the shadows stood straight and lifted something to its head. I recognized the silhouette of a horse head like the one Camden wore. I recognized the clothes I saw Susie Franklin wearing in my vision. She stepped out of the green and walked toward Camden. For all his bluster with us, the ninny cowered away from his victim.

"You ain't real. You ain't real. No. You ain't real. No. You ain't real," he chanted, like the words would change what we could all see happening.

The black opal's magic simultaneously burned and froze my skin as it passed into me and used whatever supernatural power I had to fuel it. Dizziness filled my head, and fatigue pressed on me.

Four more shadows became visible within the green haze, two big ones and two little ones. *The family Camden killed.* They all put on horse heads before stepping into the bathroom to stand behind Susie Franklin. A couple dressed in biker clothes stepped out of the green haze wearing bunny-horse heads atop their black leather outfits. The last figure to come forth was the dark-haired woman I saw reaching for me when Camden first pulled us into this piss palace. She joined her fellow victims in front of Camden. He dropped to his knees. Blubbering sounds issued from his bunny-horse head, and he ripped it off.

His forever young face shone with sweat, eyes bugging in terror. His pale lips trembled. "No, no, no." He put his hands over his eyes. "This can't happen. I killed you all. You can't hurt me. Not ever. I own you."

"You're wrong, Camden." Susie Franklin's voice was harsh and ugly like maybe her throat was full of dirt. "Anything can happen. Ain't that what you said right before you cut out my eyes?"

The father of the family Camden slaughtered stepped forward. "Before, you set the stage."

"Now, it's our turn." This came from the motorcycle couple, who spoke in unison.

A lone bathroom stall appeared behind Camden, and an invisible force pulled him into it. Chains appeared from nowhere and lashed themselves to him, hoisting him above the toilet. Camden opened his mouth so wide he looked like a snake with its jaw unhinged. A long, ugly howl issued from him. The sound raised the hair on the back of my neck. The human monster's chest first caved in and then opened. Black ichor splattered onto the floor.

I might have felt sorry for him, but karma comes back to bite us all. Especially evil cat-and-kid killers like Camden DeVoss.

"Let's go," I whispered to Mysti.

She grabbed my free hand in one hand and Griff's in her other. Together we fled the horror chamber. Camden's screams followed us into the parking lot.

"We're still stuck." Griff kicked the white brick wall of the restroom.

"Maybe not." I squeezed the black opal, begging for a little more help, and a crack appeared in the flawless asphalt. From it issued a white light.

"What if we die if we go into the light?" Griff bit his lip as he stared at the choice in front of him.

"What if we don't?" I had no idea what would happen, but I knew I couldn't listen to the sounds coming from the bathroom any more. I took the first step toward the white light. My friends followed.

An instant later, we were back in Lewis DeVoss's barn. Camden's body had gone ramrod straight, and he was about to slide out of his wheelchair. His eyes rolled up, showing whites, and foam came out of his mouth. Griff, Mysti, and I, still chained to our chairs, could do nothing but watch the spectacle.

"He's having a seizure," DeVoss screamed. "He'll die." The old man ran to his son's aid. Camden seized one last time and went still. Urine soaked the front of his khaki pants. DeVoss turned to face us, nostrils flaring, his lips twisted. "You pieces of shit killed my boy. Last family I had." The old man pushed himself to his feet, knees cracking and popping. He walked over to a wall of tools and took down a huge, bloodstained mallet and came toward us. Suddenly, I knew what the old man did with Camden's victims once his son was done.

My heart thundered in my chest, but it wasn't from fear. Fury shook through me that we went through the whole mess and escaped Camden's dream sphere only to have this sorry old bastard do us in like pigs at slaughter time. He stopped in front of me and raised the mallet over his head.

"Your mother was a useless whore. So was your wife." I gritted the words through my teeth and then spat at him. Mysti gasped next to me, but I didn't even turn my head. Didn't matter.

DeVoss's face contorted, and he leaned forward, muscles tensing, getting ready to bring the mallet down on the top of my head. I fumed at how crappy of an end it was.

A car door slammed outside the workshop. DeVoss jumped like he'd been prodded in the ass with an ice pick.

"Mr. DeVoss? You in there?" a voice called through the closed door. "It's Ollie Bickley. 'Member me? Me 'n Camden was friends."

"Help us, Ollie." I screamed so hard it hurt my throat.

DeVoss took up his stance again, obviously determined to brain me before Ollie got inside. The rolling door rose, squealing on its track as Ollie forced it to go faster. The little man ran in, pointing a tactical rifle at Lewis DeVoss. Griff had been right. It was guns after all. Ollie ran to the back of the barn and stopped several feet from DeVoss's left side.

"Stop right there, Mr. DeVoss. Put that mallet on down." Ollie danced foot to foot, eyes wild.

DeVoss grunted and raised the mallet again. The gunshots were so loud they shook me in my chair.

Lewis DeVoss jerked as each bullet penetrated him, his face slackening with surprise. He staggered sideways and dropped the mallet to clutch at his right side. The mallet thumped harmlessly on the dirt floor in front of me. Red blossoms appeared on DeVoss's shirt, soaking through the fabric and spreading fast. The old man dropped to his knees and fixed his hate-filled gaze on me. His mouth worked, but no words came out. Instead, thick, dark blood issued forth and slid down his chin. He listed sideways and fell into a clump.

Ollie turned to us, still holding the gun in his hand. "I can't go back to jail. I just can't."

"You won't," Griff said. "Get us loose. There's a bolt cutter over there on the wall."

Ollie helped Griff first. He went to the SUV and hunted down my cellphone while Ollie cut Mysti and me loose.

He handed me the cellphone. "Peri Jean, call your friend Rainey Bruce."

Rainey waited three rings to pick up. "What is it, Peri Jean? I'm busy."

I told her, and there was such a long pause, I thought the call had dropped.

"You have *got* to be kidding me. Can't you go anywhere, do anything, without getting into a big, ugly mess?"

"But can you help this guy? He saved my life." I let myself whine. With Rainey, wheedling was a necessity.

"I ought to let you rot out there. Where did you say you are? Nazareth? It's a damn dot on the map."

"Put her on speaker," Griff said. I did.

"Ms. Bruce? This is Griffin Reed, Reed Investigations. I remember watching you get crowned Miss Texas. I had a calendar with your picture—"

"Mr. Reed, please cut the crap. I'm a businesswoman, not some silly girl. All I care about is whether you have money to pay my fees."

"Name your figure, and I'll wire it to you within the hour," Griff said.

Rainey named a figure, and Griff agreed without missing a beat. I felt sick thinking about that many dollars.

"Nobody's ever gonna believe Mr. DeVoss helped Camden kill people." Ollie bellyached more than any woman I'd ever seen. No wonder his wife dumped him.

"Who is that?" Rainey snapped.

"Your new client," I said.

"The authorities won't need much convincing once they see all the bodies buried on the property," Griff said.

"We'll never find them." I stared at the two dead bodies on the floor, half waiting for one of them to get up and walk again. "Old DeVoss said he didn't even know where they were."

"I probably haven't told you how I got started investigating missing persons." Griff walked over to DeVoss's welder and grabbed two of the rods. "I'm a grave dowser."

———

"I don't believe in grave dowsing or none of that other kind of crap." The sheriff had a mean glint in his piggy eyes.

"What's it going to hurt if you let us try?" Griff held out both hands with the palms up. "You know it'll shorten your investigation, cost you less money. Plus, if we clear up all these missing persons cases in one swoop—"

"Don't get too far ahead of yourself there, Hollywood." The sheriff, whose name tag read Firth, held up a calloused hand. "You say Mr. DeVoss caused you to wreck your vehicle, chained you up in those chairs, admitted he killed Susie Franklin, and was gonna kill you too. I ain't got nobody's word but yours to go on."

"It'll take thirty minutes of your time to see if I'm wrong," Griff said.

"I'd like to see what this young man has to show us." A tall man with a head of thick, wavy white hair and a matching beard approached us.

"Now, Mayor Knightley, there wasn't no reason for you to come out here," said Sheriff Firth.

"But I'm here now. Samuel Franklin was my third cousin. Susie was blood kin. If we've a chance to recover her body without a lot of hide and seek, I'm all for it." Mayor Knightley scanned the acres of pasture surrounding us. "Even if I have to go with 'em myself."

Sheriff Firth grumbled and mumbled, but Mayor Knightley had some serious pull. Ten minutes later, we set out walking. Mysti and I had to carry the shovels. My neck screamed with about every third step, and the bad spot on my back where I'd been kicked by a real mean woman started to get stiff, but I wouldn't let myself show pain.

Griff bent each welding rod so a short piece stuck down for him to hold onto. He held the rods at chest level sticking straight out. Mayor Knightley stuck close and watched Griff with interest. The sheriff shook his head.

"Spent all forty years of my career in law enforcement and never thought I'd have to go along with something like this." He gave Mysti a sidelong glance and huffed. Then he sped up and walked a little ahead of us, hands jammed onto his hips.

My first impulse was to smart off, but I knew better than to let my inner jerk out of its bottle. I could help more if I figured out a way to speed this up. Rightly or wrongly, Sheriff Firth wasn't going to have any patience with this process. If Griff didn't find the bodies, he wouldn't get the bonuses from the victims' families. Might sound like a chicken shit reason to do other folks a good turn, but this was how Griff made a living. I tapped Mysti and whispered in her ear. "I'm going to see if I can contact any of the spirits."

She nodded and waved me off. I slipped away from the group and stood next to a watering tank and pretended to enjoy the view of the huge blue sky dotted with a few silver-white clouds. The group moved several feet into the distance. I knew it was time.

I accessed the power of the black opal and closed my eyes, pushing my conscious deep inside my mind and body to find my magic. The air around me grew cold. My eyes snapped open. I peered around, expecting to see Susie or one of the other ghosts from the rest stop bathroom. But the world was the same as when I started, other than the cooler temperature.

Then I heard the ravens calling. I turned a slow circle until I saw the black forms peppering the sky, their wings almost purple in the bright sunlight. The birds swooped and dove around a half circle of huge live oak trees. It had to be the spot. I took off running, jerking my neck around in a way it didn't like. I caught up to Griff and motioned them to follow me. Sheriff Firth grumped, but the others went willingly enough.

Soon as we crossed into the grove, Griff's dowsing rods crossed into an X.

"This is it," Griff breathed. He walked the grove. Each time he uncrossed his rods, they crossed again.

Sheriff Firth crossed his arms over his chest and glowered at me.

"How'd you know to come over here?" His gaze bored into me, probing, trying to intimidate. If I hadn't dated a cop for almost a year, Firth would have made me shake in my boots.

"You know what I do for Mr. Reed, Sheriff?" I stared right back at him, meeting his eyes, refusing to back down.

He shrugged in response.

"I'm a medium. I see ghosts." I'd keep my damn mouth shut about the ravens alerting me.

Griff took a shovel from Mysti and started digging. I stuck my own shovel in the dirt, but the sheriff pushed me aside and started his own excavation. Normally, I'd have taken his dismissal as an insult, an implication a woman couldn't do hard work, but today I hurt too damn bad to care. I went to stand next to Mysti.

"Did Susie's ghost show you where to go?" She leaned very close to me and spoke in a whisper.

"The ravens," I said. "Don't you see them?" I gestured at the sky where the birds performed air acrobatics right above us.

Mysti raised her gaze to the sky and did a slow circle. She turned back to me and slowly shook her head. Anxiety formed a hot ball in my chest. How stupid would I make Griff look if there was nothing in this grove? I crossed my arms over my chest and wished for a cigarette.

"Hold it, hold it," Sheriff Firth yelled. "I think I've found something."

Mysti and I rushed over in time to see him carefully scraping dirt off a burlap sack. The sack was so old and rotten it disintegrated, and a dull, dirty bone peeked through. The sheriff's big hands pushed more dirt away until he revealed a human jaw.

He stood and swayed lightly on his feet. "I need to make a phone call." He took out his cellphone and told someone to bring some crime scene tape and something to mark grave locations. He ended the call. A few minutes later, a loud engine sped toward us. A Sheriff's cruiser came into view.

"Mr. Reed, can you estimate how many people are

buried out here?" If Sheriff Firth was embarrassed at having to eat his disbelief, he didn't show it.

"Let me see," Griff said. Over the next few minutes, he located thirty graves. Sheriff Firth grimly marked each one. He declared the area a crime scene and told us to scram. Griff mentioned the reward money to Sheriff Firth, who rolled his eyes. Mayor Knightley, who took us back to the SUV, assured Griff he'd be a witness to how the bodies were recovered.

"Boy, this thing'll never run again." Mayor Knightley stood next to Griff in front of the SUV. He was probably right. The SUV's front was mashed in and to one side. It reminded me of a cowboy with a dip of snuff.

Grief crossed Griff's face like a storm cloud on a windy day, and he blew out a sigh.

"You'll ride with us," Mysti said.

"Hell, no." The mayor waved her off. "I'll give him a loaner off my car lot. Come on. We'll go take care of it now."

Mayor Knightley got Griff set up with a loaner. We rode in it back to the motel, grabbed our gear, and checked out. Mysti loaded our bags into her trunk, a frown on her face.

"You hurting from the wreck?" I picked up the last suitcase and handed it to her.

"Yeah, but it's nothing my pain relieving ointment and a good massage won't cure." Her gaze settled on Griff, who stood next to his loaner sedan, speaking animatedly into his cellphone. His death's door declaration of love came back to me. All of a sudden, I knew what had Mysti's undies in a twist.

"We still have to give Margaret Franklin our final report. Why don't you ride with Griff, and I'll follow you two over there?"

Instead of answering, Mysti ran over and clambered into the nondescript loaner. I slid into the driver's seat of her Toyota and waited. A few minutes later, I followed Griff out of the motel parking lot. I hoped I'd never see the rundown place again. I stared at the car's back window all the way to Margaret Franklin's neighborhood. It was so darkly tinted, I couldn't tell if Mysti and Griff were arguing or talking things over. I liked them both and hoped it was the latter.

Griff parked at the curb in front of Margaret's house, and I eased in behind him and shut off the engine, climbing out and pocketing the keys. I studied both Griff's and Mysti's faces for indication of how things went. Both had on their bland but friendly professional demeanors. Griff knocked on the door. Margaret opened it so fast, she must have been standing on the other side waiting.

"Pete—I mean, Mayor Knightley—called me a few minutes ago. They've found Susie's body." She threw her arms around Griff. He returned her hug, smiling. She turned to Mysti, gave her the same treatment, and then settled on me. She pulled me into a Chantilly Lace scented hug and whispered, "Thank you, sweetie," in my ear.

"If you don't mind me asking," Griff said, "how do they know it's Susie?"

"Her bag was buried with her. It had a little metal ID

tag on it." Margaret's lips trembled. "After all I went through, she was right there. Did Lewis DeVoss kill her?"

"Better let the sheriff assign blame, Mrs. Franklin." Griff glanced first at Mysti, then at me. I nodded to show I understood. We'd never get a law enforcement agency to understand what really happened. Lewis DeVoss deserved the blame as much as Camden.

Margaret signed the form ending her contract with Griff and paid him. She hugged us all again and saw us to the door.

"I hate to throw y'all out, but I got a real nice couple coming to look at the house in a few minutes." She gave us an apologetic curtsey.

"No problem," Mysti said. "We need to get on the road anyway."

"Good luck on selling." I knew it had to be hard, selling a place so full of memories. In a way, it made me think of the house I grew up in, the one I'd shared with Memaw. With her dead, letting go of the house where we'd lived together seemed inconceivable.

I walked toward Mysti's car, but Griff's voice stopped me.

"Peri Jean? Come over here for a minute." He didn't just sound serious. He sounded like a boss.

I walked over there, feet dragging, preparing myself for rejection. Griff stood in the open driver's side door, Mysti next to him. Both wore big grins.

"Welcome to Reed Investigations." He grabbed my hand and gave it a hard shake. "You're officially one of my contractors. When I need a medium's services, I'll be calling you. Your payment for this job will be in the mail tomorrow."

I reeled backward, unable to process his words at first. I glanced at Mysti for confirmation.

"You're in. You're one of us." She pulled me into a tight hug.

"But won't I be taking jobs away from you?"

"No. You'll free me up to do other things for Griff and to take more jobs for my own business."

"Mysti and I are going to be working more closely anyway," Griff said.

"I'm planning a move to Houston so we can be together." Mysti's smile nearly made me tear up. I couldn't have been happier for her.

"This long distance stuff is crazy." Griff swallowed hard. I couldn't tell if it was nerves or emotion choking him up.

"My kind of business can probably make more money in a bigger city, so it makes sense on several levels." Mysti smiled at me. Things had worked out for her with Griff after all.

"Thanks, Griff," I said.

"Don't get too excited. I won't be calling every week. I promise I'll make it worth your while financially when I do call." He waved me off. I walked away and climbed into the driver's seat of Mysti's car so she could say goodbye to Griff in private.

Pulling down the sun visor, I took a long hard look at myself. My dark eyes were alight with excitement. Even if Griff only called me to work for him once in a blood moon, it was a start. Stepping into a new way of living my life, of being me, especially when it was one I ran from my whole life, was like learning how to walk all over again. I was going to have to make up my mind to take baby steps. As long as I kept moving forward, it was all progress, right?

You, Peri Jean Mace, are officially a medium-for-hire, even if it's only sometimes. My appearance didn't change, but inside it felt like I did.

Keep reading for a sample of the next Peri Jean Mace
Ghost Thriller.

FORBIDDEN HIGHWAY (EXCERPT)

PERI JEAN MACE GHOST THRILLERS #5

A bloody smudge of dawn streaked across the autumn sky, marking the meeting of day and night. The abandoned wreck of Priscilla Herrera's cabin came into silvery focus. I stubbed out my cigarette and exhaled a cloud of bluish smoke. It was time.

I lit the kerosene lantern and stepped inside the cabin. My ancestor lived in this one room shack until the day a lynch mob dragged her away to be hanged for practicing witchcraft. I couldn't help but wonder if I'd end up the same way, especially as I delved deeper into the world of magic. It didn't matter at the moment. In order to move forward with my search for the Mace Treasure, I needed to speak with Priscilla's spirit.

Despite my numerous attempts to contact her, she'd been silent since the day I found out who really murdered my father. I hoped calling her spirit in the place where she lived and raised her children would get her communicating again. The Mace Treasure would remain lost to me without her help.

I set the lantern on a windowsill and looked over the supplies I'd set up in the pitch darkness while I waited for dawn. *I sure hope I brought everything.* Mysti Whitebyrd, my mentor in all things magic, warned me this method of contacting my ancestor didn't allow for careless mistakes. My need to find the Mace Treasure before another evil treasure hunter hurt me or my friends made it a necessary risk. I scanned over my supplies one more time. My breath caught.

The list of instructions. A bolt of panic shot through my chest. Had I left it at home? If so, I'd have to start over tomorrow. The spell had to be done at dawn. "No exceptions," Mysti said.

I dug through my crummy, discount store backpack. No sign of it. I shuffled through my memory. Did I recall the chant to call a circle? The details of the spell itself? Hell, no. I hadn't done it enough times. Maybe I wasn't ready for this, even though Mysti swore I was.

A memory of carefully folding my notes and putting them in my front pocket popped into my mind. I halted my frantic search and leaned my head back. If I couldn't do this without my notes, what the hell did I think I was doing?

I pulled the notes out of my pocket and scanned over Mysti's fat cursive and my spiky notations. At the very end bottom of the paper, I noticed something I hadn't before. Mysti had left me one final order. *Do not chicken out. This is the only way to learn. I love you and believe in you.*

Time to get this show on the road. I took a deep breath and began the process of centering myself.

Feet shoulder width apart and arms spread wide, I imagined roots growing out of my feet, passing through the boards on which I stood, and quickening in the soil below the cabin. I breathed deep again and focused on finding the grains of magic mixed into the particles of sand, the pieces of root, and below that, the water connecting everything. The magic seeped into me, its current tickling against my skin until it found the black opal necklace. The gemstone warmed and delivered a pinprick of electricity into my skin. We were both ready. Time to cast the circle.

I had trouble remembering the method Mysti used for calling a circle. She encouraged me to create my own way. She gifted me with my own athame, which still looked like a funky little pirate's dagger to me, to use in the process. "Practice, practice, practice," she said. Gripping the black metal handle of the dagger in my right hand, I started at the north point of the circle and went sunwise—or deosil as Mysti liked to call it—around it three times, using a chant I cobbled together from examples.

"I call upon Water to nourish my need,

I call upon Earth to strengthen my plea,

I call upon Sky to bless me this night,

I call upon Fire to augment these rites

I call to the ancients three times three—" I stopped, unable to remember what to say next, and grabbed the sheet of notes. Maybe it wouldn't hurt to read off it.

"I call to the spirits alive in me,

I call for their aid, their wisdom to guide,
I call for protection, their strength will abide
I call upon powers residing in me,
Let no evil enter, so mote it be." My final words echoed in the still dawn. A raven's caw answered me, raising the fine hairs on my arms.

I set the athame on the two-by-four serving as my altar and poured an offering of cornmeal and rum onto a pewter plate. Next to the plate, I set a picture of Priscilla Herrera herself, young and beautiful, showing off her tattoos in an age when women didn't show much skin, much less have tattoos. A mini treasure chest Priscilla used to curse the Mace Treasure went next to the picture. Her spell book went next to that. On the other side of the book, I set a bowl filled with dirt from around the cabin with a birthday candle stuck in the middle. The ancestor altar was complete. I hoped it was enough.

I opened a jar of black paint, took up the cheap paint-brush I'd bought at the discount store, and made the first line of the sigil Mysti's instructions said to draw on the plank floor.

A current came from nowhere and fluttered over my skin. The air dripped power, its chilled weight draping over me and sinking into me. A metallic taste filled my mouth. My heart thudded heavily, jarring me. I drew in deep breaths. *Stay calm. Stay calm. Keep drawing.* I made more strokes with the paintbrush.

A hum filled my head, swimming around until dizzi-ness rippled my vision. I kept drawing. The hum increased with each stroke until my teeth ached from the vibration. The sigil finished, I put down the brush. *Moment of truth.*

I picked up my cigarette lighter and spoke the words Mysti taught me. "I request the honor of Priscilla Herrera's presence when I light this candle."

I thumbed my lighter and touched the flame to the birthday candle. The hum in my head intensified, vibrating in my teeth. I clenched my jaw and clapped my hands to my ears. The air around me cooled. The first currents of panic threaded their way through me.

This wasn't what Mysti said would happen. I glanced at the sigil and realized I'd drawn it upside down. I reached out to paint over it, to correct it, to do something. I wasn't fast enough.

The oil lamps went out. I sucked in a panicked lungful of air. The flickering light of the birthday candle grew, leaping taller and blazing brighter and brighter until it burned my eyes, forcing me to drop my gaze. The heavy air seeped deep into my body, down where all my fears and self-doubts hid. The candle winked out.

"Oh, shit." My voice sounded like the squeak of a mouse trapped by a mean tomcat.

A frosty wind gusted through the pitch-black room. My clothes flapped around me, reminding me of the way flags sound on a windy day. The wind pulled harder, separating my consciousness from my body and spiriting it away into the morning mist.

I settled in a dim place, one where the still air smelled stagnant and damp. A match hissed, and the smell of sulfur overrode the other odors. A flame appeared in the darkness and moved a few inches. The flickering light paused, and a candle glowed to life a few feet in front of me. My eyes slowly adjusted to the light, revealing a figure sitting across from me. I recognized the sharp chin and high cheekbones right away. Priscilla Herrera had answered my call her own way, maybe punishing me for messing up so spectacularly with the spell.

She leaned forward, getting ready to speak. The black opal heated. The gemstone's magic would allow me to hear my great-great-great-grandmother's voice, but it would draw my energy in return.

"Not a bad way to get my attention. You're improving." Priscilla Herrera leaned toward the candle and narrowed her eyes at me. "But it's still not enough."

"I-I-I..." Fear jammed up my words. This wasn't one of those sweet grannies who handed out milk and cookies. Priscilla Herrera would scare me into doing things her way. She would hurt me if she deemed it necessary. "I-I need the spelling stones to remove the curse from the treasure. They're wherever your earthly remains are buried. Can you—"

"Hear this, granddaughter." She pointed one finger at me, and I noticed even that small part of her body was adorned with tattoos. "Until you're ready to take the next step in your journey, we've nothing to discuss. Someone else needs you now." She cupped one hand under her mouth and blew out the candle.

My consciousness must not have weighed much. It fluttered away with the puff of wind Priscilla's breath created. The smell of dampness faded, replaced by the smell of woods, pine and cedar trees, and damp, freshly turned earth. I'd gone back in time, and it was night again. Footsteps pounded the ground, and ragged breaths cut dead silence. My floating consciousness sped toward the noise, and I hit the runner hard. I passed through cold, sweaty flesh and lodged somewhere deep in her mind.

Then I saw the world through her eyes, and I knew what it felt like to run from death.

———

THE RUNNER'S LEGS ACHED, the muscles like balloons filled with hot water. A needle of agony burned at her side. She clutched at it and whined deep in her throat. She had to keep running. If she stopped, she had no chance of survival. Even this slim chance of eluding her killer was better than giving up.

The black opal's magic pulsed through me in waves, grounding me in the vision. Something about this person felt familiar. *I should know who this is.* I concentrated on every sensation.

The runner's thoughts snarled in an ugly, red welt of fear and surprise. My gift would allow me to interpret them no further. Dark shadows loomed around her. She was too scared to identify them, and I couldn't use her eyes to see things she couldn't see herself.

The sensation against her bare feet drew curiosity. I would have expected a rough carpet of pine needles, thorny vines, and rocks. Instead, the ground beneath her feet felt slick, almost soft. Familiar. I filed it away for future reference.

The girl's bare toe slammed into something hard and unforgiving. She screamed and pitched forward. Her hands slammed into the soft, damp ground. She got to her knees and crawled several feet. Her head cracked against a cold wall. Weeping, she flopped over on her side. The will to live left her body. An emptiness replaced it. She stared at the glittering stars and waited to die.

"Least the stupid bitch went to the right place." The flat twang froze the blood in my veins. The speaker laughed, a high whinnying sound. *Me-he-he-he.*

My consciousness tightened itself into a scared ball. I would have screamed had I been inside my body. That voice. I'd hoped to never hear it again. Its owner was languishing comatose in a prison hospital somewhere I didn't know or care about. This had to be a memory. No way he'd been let out to play his awful games again. I wanted out of this vision.

I concentrated on the part of me inside this scared, doomed girl, finding its limits and edges. Gathering myself, I gently pulled myself away from the girl. At first, it seemed to work. I quit feeling her emotions. Her tired muscles no longer ached as though they were my own. I pictured Priscilla Herrera's cabin, imagined my physical body there, and pushed toward it. Nothing happened. The girl's horror and pain snapped back into place.

A rough hand grabbed her arm and hauled her to her feet, squeezing so hard the muscle felt like it might pop right out of the skin. The girl shook, her frayed nerves nearly making her convulse.

"The paint can," said Michael Gage.

He can't be here. This must be a memory. Is this something he did to Rae before he killed her? I didn't want to see this. Why would Priscilla send me here? She loved terrifying me, but her sadism usually served a purpose. This had no purpose other than to hurt.

A paint can was thrust into the girl's hand, her fingers forcefully closed around it.

"Write what I say." A flashlight came to life, illuminating the face of a white wall. I was too scared to try to identify it, even though I knew it. "Hello, Peri Jean."

The girl stood frozen, an animal finished with the fight. A punch landed in the middle of her back. Her forehead cracked against the wall, but she was too far gone to react emotionally or to the pain. The hand jerked her to her feet again.

"Write it."

She shook the paint can and pressed the spray nozzle. Words slowly formed. Excess paint ran in thin lines, glowing like blood in the moonlight. Then it was finished.

HELLO, PERI JEAN

A white hot line burned across the girl's throat. She couldn't breathe. Hot liquid flowed down her arms and dripped to the ground, mirroring the drying paint on the wall in front of her. She brought her hands up to press at the wound. Her ebbing strength drove her to her knees, where she knelt on the soft earth, gagging. Her vision faded.

No, no, no. I don't want to be inside her mind while she dies. I gathered myself and reached for the black opal's power. One hard push, and I separated from her.

I woke on the floor of the cabin, the rough plank floor scratching against my cheek. The morning's first sunlight glowed softly through the windows. My first deep breath made me gag. The taste of blood still flooded my mouth. I rolled onto my back. The movement set my stomach tossing. Sharp bile stung my throat. *Uh-oh.* I scrabbled to my feet and hit the cabin door at a run. I crashed through the brush surrounding Priscilla Herrera's cabin and grabbed a skinny tree to hold onto while I emptied my stomach.

I trembled all over. My knees wobbled like the bones had gone to jelly. Fatigue siphoned off the last of my energy, and exhaustion settled in. I staggered a few feet away from my mess and eased down on a felled tree. Its rotted trunk squished underneath me, bringing thoughts of crawling, stinging insects, but I couldn't move any further.

Had Priscilla thrown me into that vision—or whatever it was—just to scare me? She didn't mind scaring me into doing her bidding, and she knew my deepest fears. She could torture me into insanity if she wanted.

Michael Gage's neighing giggle came back to me. Leaves rustled as something big moved through the woods. I leapt to my feet, peering into the forest's shadows, heart slamming. A shudder ripped through me, and I cast my gaze about the clearing. The sun's light, still soft and malleable, wrapped around the trees, draped itself over their limbs, and cast a glow on the dew still clinging to the leaves at my feet. I pulled a calming breath deep into my lungs.

"It's not him." I took my cigarettes out of my pocket and lit one with shaking hands. "Can't be. I beat his head in, and he's gone." The panic passed, and I stomped back to the cabin and packed up my altar. As I shoved the garbage into a plastic grocery sack, Priscilla's words came back. *The next step on your journey.*

All this for nothing. I didn't even accomplish what I set out to do. Would I ever get the hang of using my abilities? The idea of struggling every day for the rest of my life pissed me off. I couldn't live like that.

"What the hell do you want me to do now, you mean old woman?" I yelled at the empty cabin. Silence answered me. "That's what I thought. Scare the life out of me and won't even tell me what to do."

I toted the bag to the cabin's door and got ready to make the little drop to the ground. Two invisible hands planted themselves in the middle of my back and shoved. I pitched forward, tripped over a rock, and sprawled head first into the rotted log where I'd sat and smoked after I puked. Bright lights flashed behind my eyes. I slid off the log and leaned against it.

"You mean old lady." I shouted the words, too angry to worry about my ghostly ancestor's reaction. I rubbed at my forehead where it knocked into the tree. There'd be a knot there for sure. I got my legs under me and rose again, determined to get out of this place.

A little breeze blew through the clearing, jostling the litter of leaves and fallen branches. Something glinted on the ground at my feet. I knelt to pick it up. A lighter, once mine from the looks of it.

Cold fingers crawled over my skin. The last time I came to this place someone I should have been able to trust tried to kill me. The visit before that, I watched someone kill my father on this piece of land. All because of the Mace Treasure.

Turning a slow circle, I used the location of the cabin to get my bearings. Unless I was wrong, the tree I'd conked into was the same one I, as a little tiny girl, told my father would have to be moved if he wanted to find the treasure. *Why did I tell him that?* Because Priscilla Herrera's ghost told me. Even back then, she liked fucking with me.

A glow traveled through the woods, weaving and bobbing its way toward me. I held my breath as I watched its progress. I couldn't hear footsteps crunching through the carpet of dry leaves and branches on the forest floor. Whatever was coming wasn't human. I reached into my bag and pulled out my athame. The black opal heated on my chest.

"I'm sorry." I directed my words toward the silent, dark cabin. "I do think you're a horrible, mean woman, but I shouldn't have said it out loud. Whatever you're sending... it's not necessary because I'm sorry."

The bobbing light hovered a few feet from me now. I remembered the spooky stories Mysti Whitebyrd and her boyfriend Griff Reed told me about supernatural beings they'd battled. I wasn't ready for this. I didn't know what to do. The bobbing light came close enough to touch. It faded, and in its place stood my daddy.

"Daddy!" I whispered.

My daddy, Paul Mace, forever twenty-four and impossibly handsome, smiled at me. He came to stand at my side and pointed at the sky. Bruise colored clouds billowed over the clear morning sky. Lightning threaded through them. Thunder grumbled, and the wind picked up, swaying the tops of the tall pine trees. The whisper of the rough pine needles scraping together filled the clearing.

A frigid arm fell over my shoulders, holding me in place. "Storm coming." My father's voice faded, scratching and buzzing like a distant radio station. "Gotta do...what she says...figure it out."

Rain rushed toward us, a silver wall hissing and pounding in the trees. It peppered its way across the old homesite and stung my skin like icy needles. I turned to speak to my daddy's ghost, but he was already gone. I ran for my Nova, already soaked by the time I jumped inside. Teeth chattering, I took out my cellphone. There was a message from Tubby Tubman saying he needed to see me. I deleted it and punched in a text message to Wade Hill.

I need you.

He replied within seconds. *I know. King needs me. Can't get away.*

Can I come to you?

The bar, came the reply.

End Sample

Click here to purchase Forbidden Highway.

FORBIDDEN HIGHWAY (EXCERPT)

PERI JEAN MACE GHOST THRILLERS #5

A bloody smudge of dawn streaked across the autumn sky, marking the meeting of day and night. The abandoned wreck of Priscilla Herrera's cabin came into silvery focus. I stubbed out my cigarette and exhaled a cloud of bluish smoke. It was time.

I lit the kerosene lantern and stepped inside the cabin. My ancestor lived in this one room shack until the day a lynch mob dragged her away to be hanged for practicing witchcraft. I couldn't help but wonder if I'd end up the same way, especially as I delved deeper into the world of magic. It didn't matter at the moment. In order to move forward with my search for the Mace Treasure, I needed to speak with Priscilla's spirit.

Despite my numerous attempts to contact her, she'd been silent since the day I found out who really murdered my father. I hoped calling her spirit in the place where she lived and raised her children would get her communicating again. The Mace Treasure would remain lost to me without her help.

I set the lantern on a windowsill and looked over the supplies I'd set up in the pitch darkness while I waited for dawn. *I sure hope I brought everything.* Mysti Whitebyrd, my mentor in all things magic, warned me this method of contacting my ancestor didn't allow for careless mistakes. My need to find the Mace Treasure before another evil treasure hunter hurt me or my friends made it a necessary risk. I scanned over my supplies one more time. My breath caught.

The list of instructions. A bolt of panic shot through my chest. Had I left it at home? If so, I'd have to start over tomorrow. The spell had to be done at dawn. "No exceptions," Mysti said.

I dug through my crummy, discount store backpack. No sign of it. I shuffled through my memory. Did I recall the chant to call a circle? The details of the spell itself? Hell, no. I hadn't done it enough times. Maybe I wasn't ready for this, even though Mysti swore I was.

A memory of carefully folding my notes and putting them in my front pocket popped into my mind. I halted my frantic search and leaned my head back. If I couldn't do this without my notes, what the hell did I think I was doing?

I pulled the notes out of my pocket and scanned over Mysti's fat cursive and my spiky notations. At the very end bottom of the paper, I noticed something I hadn't before. Mysti had left me one final order. *Do not chicken out. This is the only way to learn. I love you and believe in you.*

Time to get this show on the road. I took a deep breath and began the process of centering myself.

Feet shoulder width apart and arms spread wide, I imagined roots growing out of my feet, passing through the boards on which I stood, and quickening in the soil below the cabin. I breathed deep again and focused on finding the grains of magic mixed into the particles of sand, the pieces of root, and below that, the water connecting everything. The magic seeped into me, its current tickling against my skin until it found the black opal necklace. The gemstone warmed and delivered a pinprick of electricity into my skin. We were both ready. Time to cast the circle.

I had trouble remembering the method Mysti used for calling a circle. She encouraged me to create my own way. She gifted me with my own athame, which still looked like a funky little pirate's dagger to me, to use in the process. "Practice, practice, practice," she said. Gripping the black metal handle of the dagger in my right hand, I started at the north point of the circle and went sunwise—or deosil as Mysti liked to call it—around it three times, using a chant I cobbled together from examples.

"I call upon Water to nourish my need,

I call upon Earth to strengthen my plea,

I call upon Sky to bless me this night,

I call upon Fire to augment these rites

I call to the ancients three times three—" I stopped, unable to remember what to say next, and grabbed the sheet of notes. Maybe it wouldn't hurt to read off it.

"I call to the spirits alive in me,

I call for their aid, their wisdom to guide,
I call for protection, their strength will abide
I call upon powers residing in me,
Let no evil enter, so mote it be." My final words echoed in the still dawn. A raven's caw answered me, raising the fine hairs on my arms.

I set the athame on the two-by-four serving as my altar and poured an offering of cornmeal and rum onto a pewter plate. Next to the plate, I set a picture of Priscilla Herrera herself, young and beautiful, showing off her tattoos in an age when women didn't show much skin, much less have tattoos. A mini treasure chest Priscilla used to curse the Mace Treasure went next to the picture. Her spell book went next to that. On the other side of the book, I set a bowl filled with dirt from around the cabin with a birthday candle stuck in the middle. The ancestor altar was complete. I hoped it was enough.

I opened a jar of black paint, took up the cheap paintbrush I'd bought at the discount store, and made the first line of the sigil Mysti's instructions said to draw on the plank floor.

A current came from nowhere and fluttered over my skin. The air dripped power, its chilled weight draping over me and sinking into me. A metallic taste filled my mouth. My heart thudded heavily, jarring me. I drew in deep breaths. *Stay calm. Stay calm. Keep drawing.* I made more strokes with the paintbrush.

A hum filled my head, swimming around until dizziness rippled my vision. I kept drawing. The hum increased with each stroke until my teeth ached from the vibration. The sigil finished, I put down the brush. *Moment of truth.*

I picked up my cigarette lighter and spoke the words Mysti taught me. "I request the honor of Priscilla Herrera's presence when I light this candle."

I thumbed my lighter and touched the flame to the birthday candle. The hum in my head intensified, vibrating in my teeth. I clenched my jaw and clapped my hands to my ears. The air around me cooled. The first currents of panic threaded their way through me.

This wasn't what Mysti said would happen. I glanced at the sigil and realized I'd drawn it upside down. I reached out to paint over it, to correct it, to do something. I wasn't fast enough.

The oil lamps went out. I sucked in a panicked lungful of air. The flickering light of the birthday candle grew, leaping taller and blazing brighter and brighter until it burned my eyes, forcing me to drop my gaze. The heavy air seeped deep into my body, down where all my fears and self-doubts hid. The candle winked out.

"Oh, shit." My voice sounded like the squeak of a mouse trapped by a mean tomcat.

A frosty wind gusted through the pitch-black room. My clothes flapped around me, reminding me of the way flags sound on a windy day. The wind pulled harder, separating my consciousness from my body and spiriting it away into the morning mist.

I settled in a dim place, one where the still air smelled stagnant and damp. A match hissed, and the smell of sulfur overrode the other odors. A flame appeared in the darkness and moved a few inches. The flickering light paused, and a candle glowed to life a few feet in front of me. My eyes slowly adjusted to the light, revealing a figure sitting across from me. I recognized the sharp chin and high cheekbones right away. Priscilla Herrera had answered my call her own way, maybe punishing me for messing up so spectacularly with the spell.

She leaned forward, getting ready to speak. The black opal heated. The gemstone's magic would allow me to hear my great-great-great-grandmother's voice, but it would draw my energy in return.

"Not a bad way to get my attention. You're improving." Priscilla Herrera leaned toward the candle and narrowed her eyes at me. "But it's still not enough."

"I-I-I..." Fear jammed up my words. This wasn't one of those sweet grannies who handed out milk and cookies. Priscilla Herrera would scare me into doing things her way. She would hurt me if she deemed it necessary. "I-I need the spelling stones to remove the curse from the treasure. They're wherever your earthly remains are buried. Can you—"

"Hear this, granddaughter." She pointed one finger at me, and I noticed even that small part of her body was adorned with tattoos. "Until you're ready to take the next step in your journey, we've nothing to discuss. Someone else needs you now." She cupped one hand under her mouth and blew out the candle.

My consciousness must not have weighed much. It fluttered away with the puff of wind Priscilla's breath created. The smell of dampness faded, replaced by the smell of woods, pine and cedar trees, and damp, freshly turned earth. I'd gone back in time, and it was night again. Footsteps pounded the ground, and ragged breaths cut dead silence. My floating consciousness sped toward the noise, and I hit the runner hard. I passed through cold, sweaty flesh and lodged somewhere deep in her mind.

Then I saw the world through her eyes, and I knew what it felt like to run from death.

———

THE RUNNER'S LEGS ACHED, the muscles like balloons filled with hot water. A needle of agony burned at her side. She clutched at it and whined deep in her throat. She had to keep running. If she stopped, she had no chance of survival. Even this slim chance of eluding her killer was better than giving up.

The black opal's magic pulsed through me in waves, grounding me in the vision. Something about this person felt familiar. *I should know who this is.* I concentrated on every sensation.

The runner's thoughts snarled in an ugly, red welt of fear and surprise. My gift would allow me to interpret them no further. Dark shadows loomed around her. She was too scared to identify them, and I couldn't use her eyes to see things she couldn't see herself.

The sensation against her bare feet drew curiosity. I would have expected a rough carpet of pine needles, thorny vines, and rocks. Instead, the ground beneath her feet felt slick, almost soft. Familiar. I filed it away for future reference.

The girl's bare toe slammed into something hard and unforgiving. She screamed and pitched forward. Her hands slammed into the soft, damp ground. She got to her knees and crawled several feet. Her head cracked against a cold wall. Weeping, she flopped over on her side. The will to live left her body. An emptiness replaced it. She stared at the glittering stars and waited to die.

"Least the stupid bitch went to the right place." The flat twang froze the blood in my veins. The speaker laughed, a high whinnying sound. *Me-he-he-he.*

My consciousness tightened itself into a scared ball. I would have screamed had I been inside my body. That voice. I'd hoped to never hear it again. Its owner was languishing comatose in a prison hospital somewhere I didn't know or care about. This had to be a memory. No way he'd been let out to play his awful games again. I wanted out of this vision.

I concentrated on the part of me inside this scared, doomed girl, finding its limits and edges. Gathering myself, I gently pulled myself away from the girl. At first, it seemed to work. I quit feeling her emotions. Her tired muscles no longer ached as though they were my own. I pictured Priscilla Herrera's cabin, imagined my physical body there, and pushed toward it. Nothing happened. The girl's horror and pain snapped back into place.

A rough hand grabbed her arm and hauled her to her feet, squeezing so hard the muscle felt like it might pop right out of the skin. The girl shook, her frayed nerves nearly making her convulse.

"The paint can," said Michael Gage.

He can't be here. This must be a memory. Is this something he did to Rae before he killed her? I didn't want to see this. Why would Priscilla send me here? She loved terrifying me, but her sadism usually served a purpose. This had no purpose other than to hurt.

A paint can was thrust into the girl's hand, her fingers forcefully closed around it.

"Write what I say." A flashlight came to life, illuminating the face of a white wall. I was too scared to try to identify it, even though I knew it. "Hello, Peri Jean."

The girl stood frozen, an animal finished with the fight. A punch landed in the middle of her back. Her forehead cracked against the wall, but she was too far gone to react emotionally or to the pain. The hand jerked her to her feet again.

"Write it."

She shook the paint can and pressed the spray nozzle. Words slowly formed. Excess paint ran in thin lines, glowing like blood in the moonlight. Then it was finished.

HELLO, PERI JEAN

A white hot line burned across the girl's throat. She couldn't breathe. Hot liquid flowed down her arms and dripped to the ground, mirroring the drying paint on the wall in front of her. She brought her hands up to press at the wound. Her ebbing strength drove her to her knees, where she knelt on the soft earth, gagging. Her vision faded.

No, no, no. I don't want to be inside her mind while she dies. I gathered myself and reached for the black opal's power. One hard push, and I separated from her.

I woke on the floor of the cabin, the rough plank floor scratching against my cheek. The morning's first sunlight glowed softly through the windows. My first deep breath made me gag. The taste of blood still flooded my mouth. I rolled onto my back. The movement set my stomach tossing. Sharp bile stung my throat. *Uh-oh.* I scrabbled to my feet and hit the cabin door at a run. I crashed through the brush surrounding Priscilla Herrera's cabin and grabbed a skinny tree to hold onto while I emptied my stomach.

I trembled all over. My knees wobbled like the bones had gone to jelly. Fatigue siphoned off the last of my energy, and exhaustion settled in. I staggered a few feet away from my mess and eased down on a felled tree. Its rotted trunk squished underneath me, bringing thoughts of crawling, stinging insects, but I couldn't move any further.

Had Priscilla thrown me into that vision—or whatever it was—just to scare me? She didn't mind scaring me into doing her bidding, and she knew my deepest fears. She could torture me into insanity if she wanted.

Michael Gage's neighing giggle came back to me. Leaves rustled as something big moved through the woods. I leapt to my feet, peering into the forest's shadows, heart slamming. A shudder ripped through me, and I cast my gaze about the clearing. The sun's light, still soft and malleable, wrapped around the trees, draped itself over their limbs, and cast a glow on the dew still clinging to the leaves at my feet. I pulled a calming breath deep into my lungs.

"It's not him." I took my cigarettes out of my pocket and lit one with shaking hands. "Can't be. I beat his head in, and he's gone." The panic passed, and I stomped back to the cabin and packed up my altar. As I shoved the garbage into a plastic grocery sack, Priscilla's words came back. *The next step on your journey.*

All this for nothing. I didn't even accomplish what I set out to do. Would I ever get the hang of using my abilities? The idea of struggling every day for the rest of my life pissed me off. I couldn't live like that.

"What the hell do you want me to do now, you mean old woman?" I yelled at the empty cabin. Silence answered me. "That's what I thought. Scare the life out of me and won't even tell me what to do."

I toted the bag to the cabin's door and got ready to make the little drop to the ground. Two invisible hands planted themselves in the middle of my back and shoved. I pitched forward, tripped over a rock, and sprawled head first into the rotted log where I'd sat and smoked after I puked. Bright lights flashed behind my eyes. I slid off the log and leaned against it.

"You mean old lady." I shouted the words, too angry to worry about my ghostly ancestor's reaction. I rubbed at my forehead where it knocked into the tree. There'd be a knot there for sure. I got my legs under me and rose again, determined to get out of this place.

A little breeze blew through the clearing, jostling the litter of leaves and fallen branches. Something glinted on the ground at my feet. I knelt to pick it up. A lighter, once mine from the looks of it.

Cold fingers crawled over my skin. The last time I came to this place someone I should have been able to trust tried to kill me. The visit before that, I watched someone kill my father on this piece of land. All because of the Mace Treasure.

Turning a slow circle, I used the location of the cabin to get my bearings. Unless I was wrong, the tree I'd conked into was the same one I, as a little tiny girl, told my father would have to be moved if he wanted to find the treasure. *Why did I tell him that?* Because Priscilla Herrera's ghost told me. Even back then, she liked fucking with me.

A glow traveled through the woods, weaving and bobbing its way toward me. I held my breath as I watched its progress. I couldn't hear footsteps crunching through the carpet of dry leaves and branches on the forest floor. Whatever was coming wasn't human. I reached into my bag and pulled out my athame. The black opal heated on my chest.

"I'm sorry." I directed my words toward the silent, dark cabin. "I do think you're a horrible, mean woman, but I shouldn't have said it out loud. Whatever you're sending... it's not necessary because I'm sorry."

The bobbing light hovered a few feet from me now. I remembered the spooky stories Mysti Whitebyrd and her boyfriend Griff Reed told me about supernatural beings they'd battled. I wasn't ready for this. I didn't know what to do. The bobbing light came close enough to touch. It faded, and in its place stood my daddy.

"Daddy!" I whispered.

My daddy, Paul Mace, forever twenty-four and impossibly handsome, smiled at me. He came to stand at my side and pointed at the sky. Bruise colored clouds billowed over the clear morning sky. Lightning threaded through them. Thunder grumbled, and the wind picked up, swaying the tops of the tall pine trees. The whisper of the rough pine needles scraping together filled the clearing.

A frigid arm fell over my shoulders, holding me in place. "Storm coming." My father's voice faded, scratching and buzzing like a distant radio station. "Gotta do...what she says...figure it out."

Rain rushed toward us, a silver wall hissing and pounding in the trees. It peppered its way across the old homesite and stung my skin like icy needles. I turned to speak to my daddy's ghost, but he was already gone. I ran for my Nova, already soaked by the time I jumped inside. Teeth chattering, I took out my cellphone. There was a message from Tubby Tubman saying he needed to see me. I deleted it and punched in a text message to Wade Hill.

I need you.

He replied within seconds. *I know. King needs me. Can't get away.*

Can I come to you?

The bar, came the reply.

End Sample
Purchase Forbidden Highway from your favorite bookseller.
ISBN: 978-1-947462-11-3

Visit Catie's website:
www.catierhodes.com

Find Catie on Facebook:
http://www.facebook.com/catierhodesauthor

Follow Catie on Book Bub.
https://www.bookbub.com/authors/catie-rhodes

Join Catie's email list:
http://smarturl.it/lrdenewsletter

ABOUT THE AUTHOR

Catie Rhodes writes southern-fried urban fantasy with a strong dose of horror and a side dish of humor.

She is the author of the Peri Jean Mace Ghost Thrillers. Her short stories have appeared in *Tales From The Mist, Let's Scare Cancer to Death, and Allegories of the Tarot.*

Catie was born and raised behind the pine curtain in East Texas. She comes from a family of world champion liars.

Their tall tales molded Catie into a purveyor of her own brand of lies and legends. One day, she found the courage to start writing down her stories. It changed her life forever.

Catie Rhodes lives steps from the Sam Houston National Forest with her long-suffering husband and her armpit terrorist of a little dog.

Find Catie online:
www.catierhodes.com